The Coming of the Robots

The Coming of the Robots

EDITED, AND WITH AN INTRODUCTION, BY

SAM MOSKOWITZ

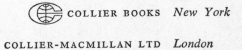 COLLIER BOOKS *New York*

COLLIER-MACMILLAN LTD *London*

To

Otto O. Binder

Popularizer of the

"modern" robot

Acknowledgments

I, ROBOT by Eando Binder: Copyright 1938 by the Ziff-Davis Publishing Company for *Amazing Stories*. Reprinted by permission of the author.

HELEN O'LOY by Lester Del Rey: Copyright 1938 by Street & Smith Publications, Inc. Reprinted by permission of the author and Scott Meredith Literary Agency.

THE LOST MACHINE by John Wyndham: Copyright 1932 by the Teck Publishing Corp. for *Amazing Stories*. Reprinted by permission of the author and Scott Meredith Literary Agency.

RUNAROUND by Isaac Asimov: Copyright 1942 by Street & Smith Publications, Inc. for *Astounding Science-Fiction*. Reprinted by permission of the author.

EARTH FOR INSPIRATION by Clifford D. Simak: Copyright 1941 by Better Publications, Inc. for *Thrilling Wonder Stories*. Reprinted by permission of the author.

LOST MEMORY by Peter Phillips: Copyright 1952 by the Galaxy Publishing Corp. for *Galaxy Science Fiction*. Reprinted by permission of Scott Meredith Literary Agency.

REX by Harl Vincent: Copyright 1934 by Street & Smith Publications, Inc. for *Astounding Stories*. Reprinted by permission of the Forrest J. Ackerman Literary Agency.

TRUE CONFESSION by F. Orlin Tremaine: Copyright 1939 by Better Publications, Inc. for *Thrilling Wonder Stories*. Reprinted by permission of Mrs. De Witt C. Tremaine.

DERELICT by Raymond Z. Gallun: Copyright 1935 by Street & Smith Publications, Inc. for *Astounding Stories*. Reprinted by permission of Rogers Terrill Literary Agency.

MISFIT by Michael Fischer: Copyright 1935 by Gernsback Publications Inc. for *Science-Fiction Plus*. Reprinted by permission of the copyright owners.

Contents

Introduction

IT HAS BEEN SAID, with considerable justice, that the age of robots is already here. Aircraft take off, fly, and land with no pilots; great industrial plants, frequently many square miles in area, function like great cities with no human workers in sight; giant electronic computers do the work of a thousand mathematicians in minutes and even play outstanding games of chess against human champions. In a very real sense, all these devices are robots, automatically doing the work of human beings, but they are not what the man in the street thinks of when he uses the term.

The man-like machine, preferably with two legs and two arms, with photoelectric cells for eyes and an electronic brain remains today and may always remain the symbol of the robot to the general public. The public thinks of a robot as a *mechanical man*, and, with two qualified exceptions, these are the kind of robots the stories in this book are about.

There have been robots of one sort or another in

9

fiction for well over 100 years, and references to mechanical men appear in records more than 2,000 years old, but the word itself, as an addition to the English language, is relatively new. It first appeared in the play *R. U. R.* by Karel Căpek, greatest of all Czechoslovakian playwrights, when that famed classic concerning the revolt of artificial men was premiered in Prague on January 26, 1921. The term was derived from the Czech word *robota*, meaning "to work."

If mechanical men are actually created in the future, their function will be to do the work formerly done by men. At first their appearance will be completely in the form of a machine, but as technology advances, a wedding of plastics and metal will result in robot devices so closely resembling humans that they will have to be marked to be distinguished.

The roots of man's conception of a robot go deep into literary history. It has been suggested that Publius Vergilius Maro, better known as Vergil, greatest poet of ancient Rome, constructed innumerable metal devices, including bronze archers to protect his premises. The variety of these stories linking Vergil with the building of robots is in itself a fascinating area of research.

These legends of Vergil, together with Ovid's masterful depiction of a statue come to life, are believed to have inspired the tales of the Golem, an artificial man constructed from clay by the Jews to serve them on the Sabbath and protect them from their enemies.

There are dozens of Golem legends, mostly from

Eastern European sources, some of them as recent as the early nineteenth century. The most famous legends of the Golem, however, emanated from sixteenth-century Prague, where such an artificial man was said to have been the servant of the famed Rabbi Judah Loew.

The Golem is unquestionably the prototype for the monster of Mary Wollstonecraft Shelley's *Frankenstein*, a work whose importance to the literary history of the mechanical man lies in its plot innovation, the concept of an artificial man turning on his creator. *Frankenstein*, like many other early robot stories, may be considered antiscientific, insofar as it equates the advancement of knowledge with disaster.

A Hungarian nobleman, Baron Kempelen of Presburg, was inadvertently responsible for the American interest in robots. An ingenious mechanic, he devised many robots that walked, actually *talked*, and performed other mechanically mystifying operations. His most famous invention was a mechanical chess player, built out of metal to resemble a turbaned Turk, which engaged men in public contests throughout Europe. He sold this invention to a German named Johann Nepomuk Maelzel in 1769. The robot subsequently toured the United States during the early part of the nineteenth century.

Edgar Allan Poe, then editor of *The Southern Literary Messenger*, with editorial offices in Richmond, Va., performed one of the most brilliant exposés of the period after reading a report on this device. With no other evidence than published descriptions of the operation of the chess player, he proved by deductive logic that the machine was a fraud operated by a left-handed midget, concealed through the use of mirrors. His exposé, published in 1836, as well as a reference to the automatic chess player included in his short story "The Thousand-and-Second Tale of Scheherazade" (1845) influenced the entire course of literature dealing with mechanical men in the United States.

The most famous derivative of Poe's analysis of the mechanical chess player was Ambrose Bierce's classic, "Moxon's Master," the story of a chess-playing robot built by a scientist, which eventually, like Frankenstein's monster, kills its master.

Poe bears some responsibility for influencing a series of dime novels (they actually sold for five cents), beginning in 1868, dealing with steam men and steam horses invented by teen-aged geniuses and used to fight Indians and highwaymen. The most famous of these stories were the inventions of a sixteen-year-old Brooklyn boy, Luis Senarens, writing under the pen name of "Noname." His most popular character, Frank Reade, Jr., embarked on a series of adventures which Senarens began chronicling in 1879 and which he continued past the turn of the century. They are remembered nostalgically, today by thousands of boys, now grown old, because of their numerous prophecies of submarines, airplanes, spaceships, helicopters, and tanks.

The Frank Reade, Jr. robots were mindless steam and electric engines shaped like men. Most of the fictional robots that followed, however, were capable of thought, much like Ambrose Bierce's thinking machine; these were always depicted as treacherous and dangerous.

This hostile characterization continued right into the era of the science fiction magazines, the first of which, *Amazing Stories*, was launched with the dateline April 1926. Until the appearance of "The Lost Machine" by John Beynon Harris in the April 1932 issue of that magazine, authors vied with one another to contrive increasingly gruesome means by which robots could turn on mankind and assume control of the world.

Feeling, perhaps, that its readers would not immediately accept the notion of a friendly machine, Harris created an advanced *Martian* robot, who gives his first-person reaction to being stranded on the much more primitive Earth. Since the appearance of that story, Harris has become much better known under the pseudonym of John Wyndham.

Authors then began to re-examine their approach to robots. Beginning with John W. Campbell, Jr., in his short story "The Last Evolution" which appeared in *Amazing Stories* for August 1932, robots were depicted as allies of future man in his losing battle against invasion from outer space.

The theme of the robot as a menace is not likely to die out, but in the future it will be necessary to give it a special note of originality to make it palatable. Harl Vincent, writing in the June 1934, *Astounding Stories*, presented "Rex," a robot surgeon of such intelligence that he seizes control of all civilization and then tries to learn the meaning of emotions, the only area in which he was not superior to the enslaved humans.

Raymond Z. Gallun in "Derelict" (*Astounding Stories*, October 1935), taking his cue from the robot in "The Lost Machine," creates a fantastically alien automaton, whose builders have long since disappeared. In contact with a grief-stricken spaceman, the robot gradually restores the man's will to live and to face reality again. This left an opening for Robert Moore Williams to bring a race of arrogant robots back from a far star system, in the very distant future ("Robot's Return," *Astounding Science-Fiction*, August 1938) to the ruins of a dead Earth. They are sobered by the knowledge that they were created by the relatively fragile flesh-and-blood men.

Psychologically the time was now ripe to launch an assault against the reader's prejudices concerning robots. Two stories, appearing within weeks of one another, deserve the lion's share of the credit. The first was "I, Robot" (*Amazing Stories*, January 1938) by Eando Binder, which reversed the plot of *Frankenstein* and showed how the public could be made to believe that a robot, in this case Adam Link, was a threat to humanity, whereas in reality his motives were more noble than those of most men.

The second was "Helen O'Loy" by Lester Del Rey (*Astounding Science-Fiction*, December 1938) wherein robot technology has advanced to the point where robots are outwardly indistinguishable from humans. This story of a female robot, designed for housekeeping purposes, who falls in love with her owner, is one of the most tender and poignant stories in science fiction.

Reader reaction was so enthusiastic to both these stories that Eando Binder carried Adam Link through innumerable sequels and even employed him in a comic-magazine continuity. Dozens of authors immediately began to explore the potential of this science fiction plot gambit, which was to become second in popularity only to the interplanetary story.

What Binder and Del Rey had done was simple. They attributed human emotions to machines and showed the problems that result when the machines' personal feelings came in conflict with their tasks.

In "True Confession," F. Orlin Tremaine, the editor who had initially purchased and published both "Rex" and "Derelict," picked up the new formula and dramatized the credibility of a robot as a witness in a murder trial.

Clifford D. Simak, employing the plot devices in "Helen O'Loy," where the "female" robot is conditioned by soap operas and trashy novels to romantic notions, has a robot of the future who reads too many stories of science fiction in which his counterparts perform heroic deeds. He runs away from home and stows away on a spaceship making its way back to ancient, dying Earth (as in "Robots Return") in search of adventure.

Of course, you can't have all those robots running helter-skelter and getting tangled up in their emotions without having some sort of check on them. The man who really brought order out of chaos was Isaac Asimov, when he propounded his Three Laws of Robotics:

1. A robot may not injure a human being, or, through inaction, allow a human being to come to harm.

2. A robot must obey the orders given it by human beings except where such orders would conflict with the First Law.

3. A robot must protect its own existence as long as such protection does not conflict with the First or Second Law.

A series of stories concerning robots, based on those laws, was written by Isaac Asimov. One of the most entertaining, "Runaround" (*Astounding Science-Fiction*, March 1942), clearly dramatizes the operation of The Three Laws of Robotics, and has the added advantage of being a robot story in an interplanetary setting.

Since Asimov postulated his robot regulations, they have either been adopted or become implicit in the robot stories of many leading science fiction writers. The careful reading of modern robot stories reveals how much they owe to these limiting factors.

The idea has not been lost on authors that, if the day arrives when robots become self-conscious personalities, it is inevitable that robot colonies, without any humans at all, may some day come into being. Such robot societies are projected in "Lost Memory," where Peter Phillips conceives a robot civilization on a world in a far galaxy, cut off so long from human contact that the robots cannot comprehend the very concept of a flesh-and-blood creature.

Of course, the humanizing of robots, while immensely popularizing that phase of science fiction, has not meant the end of good stories based on the Frankenstein-monster line. The results can often prove immensely clever, as displayed by Michael Fischer's brief but effective tale "Misfit," from *Science-Fiction Plus* for December 1953.

The reader who finds that he has thoroughly enjoyed the surprising variety of stories in this collection, in which the robot is the story's central figure, may eagerly search for more of the same in today's science fiction magazines. He will find plenty of robots, but many of them will play different roles from the ones in this volume. For today's robot is often one of the cast of characters, not necessarily the star of the show. The science fiction writer has a special problem which the writer of non-science fiction does not have. When the science fiction writer sits down at a typewriter he must not only write a good story, but *he must invent from start to finish the world in which the story takes place!* There is no map of the future, no book of its customs, laws, and problems.

A writer in a non-science fiction story need only say that his character stepped out of a Rolls-Royce and immediately the reader accepts the fact that the man is rich. He can also accomplish the same thing by saying: "The butler helped him to dress." But what will be the symbol of wealth of the man of the future? To give the impression of wealth, the science fiction writer must employ some other device, and what could be better than a chromium-plated robot tending to his master's every wish in response to electronic signals?

In a story of today, if a man escapes from prison, the reader expects him to be chased by bloodhounds. You can't have bloodhounds following a man who has escaped from a prison on Mars, but you can use a robot, equipped with detecting devices to track a man on that planet.

In a modern spy story, the secret agent, in order to get the information he wants, learns to talk, act, and dress like the people from whom he wants to get the information. But suppose you wanted to learn the secrets of the blue people of Venus who have six arms and four legs and breathe mustard gas instead of oxygen? A more practical means would be to build a robot that looked and acted like those Venusians.

The foregoing are just a few examples of what a very, very useful device the robot is to the science fiction writer.

As a result of using the robot so often and in so many ways, a strange thing has happened. Just as the camel reminds one immediately of Egypt, the skyscraper of New York, orange juice of Florida, and six-guns of the Old West, the robot has come to be associated with the *future*.

The writer, in effect, sets the mood and period of his story by introducing the robot, who may even lend it a note of *authenticity*. Once the robot was only the symbol of a Frankenstein monster; when the space rocket becomes commonplace, however, he may very well become the new symbol of science fiction!

SAM MOSKOWITZ

October 1962

The Coming of the Robots

I, Robot

Eando Binder

Eando Binder was originally the pen name of two brothers, Earl and Otto Binder, who began writing science fiction in 1932. Earl retired from writing in 1936, and all Eando Binder stories since then have been the work of Otto. By 1938 Eando Binder had become one of the three most popular writers in the field and his work began to appear outside of the science fiction magazines in Argosy *and* Action Stories. *His popularity reached its height with the introduction of a robot character named Adam Link, whose appearance in "I, Robot" was a major factor in changing the pattern of robot stories so that the robots were treated sympathetically instead of as villains. He had a facility for good characterization and plot. His talent for plotting caused him to leave science fiction in the early 1940's to write the comic strip continuities for* Captain Marvel, *whose destinies he guided for seventeen years. He is presently editor of two popular magazines of space exploration,* Space World *and* Jets and Rockets.

I, Robot

My Creation

MUCH OF WHAT HAS OCCURRED puzzles me. But I think I am beginning to understand now. You call me a monster, but you are wrong. Utterly wrong!

I will try to prove it to you, in writing. I hope I have time to finish. . . .

I will begin at the beginning. I was born, or created, six months ago, on November 3 of last year. I am a true robot. So many of you seem to have doubts. I am made of wires and wheels, not flesh and blood.

My first recollection of consciousness was a feeling of being chained, and I was. For three days before that, I had been seeing and hearing, but all in a jumble. Now, I had the urge to arise and peer more closely at the strange, moving form that I had seen so many times before me, making sounds.

The moving form was Dr. Link, my creator. He

was the only thing that moved, of all the objects within my sight. He and one other object—his dog Terry. Therefore these two objects held my interest more. I hadn't yet learned to associate movement with life.

But on this fourth day, I wanted to approach the two moving shapes and make noises at them—particularly at the smaller one. His noises were challenging, stirring. They made me want to rise and quiet them. But I was chained. I was held down by them so that, in my blank state of mind, I wouldn't wander off and bring myself to an untimely end, or harm someone unknowingly.

These things, of course, Dr. Link explained to me later, when I could dissociate my thoughts and understand. I was just like a baby for those three days—a human baby. I am not as other so-called robots were—mere automatized machines designed to obey certain commands or arranged stimuli.

No, I was equipped with a pseudo-brain that could receive *all* stimuli that human brains could. And with possibilities of eventually learning to rationalize for itself.

But for three days Dr. Link was very anxious about my brain. I was like a human baby and yet I was also like a sensitive, but unorganized, machine, subject to the whim of mechanical chance. My eyes turned when a bit of paper fluttered to the floor. But photoelectric cells had been made before capable of doing the same. My mechanical ears turned to receive sounds best from a certain direction, but any scientist could duplicate that trick with sonic relays.

The question was—did my brain, to which the eyes and ears were connected, hold on to these various impressions for future use? Did I have, in short—*memory?*

Three days I was like a newborn baby. And Dr. Link was like a worried father, wondering if his child had been born a hopeless idiot. But on the fourth day, he feared I was a wild animal. I began to make rasping sounds with my vocal apparatus, in answer to the sharp little noises Terry the dog made. I shook my swivel head at the same time and strained against my bonds.

For a while, as Dr. Link told me, he was frightened of me. I seemed like nothing so much as an enraged jungle creature, ready to go berserk. He had more than half a mind to destroy me on the spot.

But one thing changed his mind and saved me.

The little animal, Terry, barking angrily, rushed forward suddenly. It probably wanted to bite me. Dr. Link tried to call it back, but too late. Finding my smooth metal legs adamant, the dog leaped with foolish bravery in my lap, to come at my throat. One of my hands grasped it by the middle, held it up. My metal fingers squeezed too hard, and the dog gave out a pained squeal.

Instantaneously, my hand opened to let the creature escape! Instantaneously. My brain had interpreted the sound for what it was. A long chain of memory-association had worked. Three days before, when I had first been brought to life, Dr. Link had stepped on Terry's foot accidentally. The dog had squealed its pain. I had seen Dr. Link, at risk of losing his balance, instantly jerk up his foot. Terry had stopped squealing.

Terry squealed when my hand tightened. He would stop when I untightened. Memory-association. The thing psychologists call reflexive reaction. A sign of a living brain.

Dr. Link tells me he let out a cry of pure triumph. He knew at a stroke I had memory. He knew I was not a wanton monster. He knew I had a thinking organ, and a first-class one. Why? Because I had reacted *instantaneously*. You will realize what that means later.

I learned to walk in three hours. Dr. Link was still taking somewhat of a chance, unbinding my chains. He had no assurance that I would not just blunder away like a witless machine. But he knew he had to teach me to walk before I could learn to talk. The same as he knew he must bring my brain alive fully connected to the appendages and pseudo-organs it was later to use.

If he had simply disconnected my legs and arms for those first three days, my awakening brain would never have been able to use them when connected later. Do you think, if you were suddenly endowed with a third arm, that you could ever use it? Why does it take a cured paralytic so long to regain the use of his natural limbs? Mental blind spots in the brain. Dr. Link had all those strange psychological twists figured out.

Walk first. Talk next. That is the tried-and-true

rule used among humans since the dawn of their species. Human babies learn best and fastest that way. And I was a human baby in mind, if not body.

Dr. Link held his breath when I first essayed to rise. I did, slowly, swaying on my metal legs. Up in my head, I had a three-directional spirit-level electrically contacting my brain. It told me automatically what was horizontal, vertical, and oblique. My first tentative step, however, wasn't a success. My knee joints flexed in reverse order. I clattered to my knees, which fortunately were knobbed with thick protective plates so that the more delicate swiveling mechanisms behind weren't harmed.

Dr. Link says I looked up at him like a startled child might. Then I promptly began walking along on my knees, finding this easy. Children would do this more only that it hurts them. I know no hurt.

After I had roved up and down the aisles of his workshop for an hour, nicking up his furniture terribly, walking on my knees seemed completely natural. Dr. Link was in a quandary how to get me up to my full height. He tried grasping my arm and pulling me up, but my 300 pounds of weight were too much for him.

My own rapidly increasing curiosity solved the problem. Like a child discovering the thrill of added height with stilts, my next attempt to rise to my full height pleased me. I tried staying up. I finally mastered the technique of alternate use of limbs and shift of weight forward.

In a couple of hours Dr. Link was leading me up and down the gravel walk around his laboratory.

On my legs, it was quite easy for him to pull me along and thus guide me. Little Terry gamboled along at our heels, barking joyfully. The dog had accepted me as a friend.

I was by this time quite docile to Dr. Link's guidance. My impressionable mind had quietly accepted him as a necessary rein and check. I did, he told me later, make tentative movements in odd directions off the path, motivated by vague stimuli, but his firm arm pulling me back served instantly to keep me in line. He paraded up and down with me as one might with an irresponsible oaf.

I would have kept on walking tirelessly for hours, but Dr. Link's burden of years quickly fatigued him and he led me inside. When he had safely gotten me seated in my metal chair, he clicked the switch on my chest that broke the electric current giving me life. And for the fourth time I knew that dreamless non-being which corresponded to my creator's periods of sleep.

My Education

In three days I learned to talk reasonably well.

I give Dr. Link as much credit as myself. In those three days he pointed out the names of all objects in the laboratory and around. This fund of two hundred or so nouns he supplemented with as many verbs of action as he could demonstrate. Once heard and learned, a word never again was forgotten or obscured to me. Instantaneous comprehension. Photographic memory. Those things I had.

It is difficult to explain. Machinery is precise, unvarying. I am a machine. Electrons perform their tasks instantaneously. Electrons motivate my metallic brain.

Thus, with the intelligence of a child of five at the end of those three days, I was taught to read by Dr. Link. My photoelectric eyes instantly grasped the connection between speech and letter, as my mentor pointed them out. Thought-association filled in the gaps of understanding. I perceived without delay that the word "lion," for instance, pronounced in its peculiar way, represented a live animal crudely pictured in the book. I have never seen a lion. But I would know one the instant I did.

From primers and first-readers I graduated in less than a week to adult books. Dr. Link laid out an extensive reading course for me in his large library. It included fiction as well as factual matter. Into my receptive, retentive brain began to be poured a fund of information and knowledge never before equaled in that short period of time.

There are other things to consider besides my "birth" and "education." First of all the housekeeper. She came in once a week to clean up the house for Dr. Link. He was a recluse, lived by himself, cooked for himself—retired on an annuity from an invention years before.

The housekeeper had seen me in the process of construction in the past years, but only as an inanimate caricature of a human body. Dr. Link should have known better. When the first Saturday of my life came around, he forgot it was the day she came.

He was absorbedly pointing out to me that "to run" meant to go faster than "to walk."

"Demonstrate," Dr. Link asked as I claimed understanding.

Obediently, I took a few slow steps before him. "Walking," I said. Then I retreated a ways and lumbered forward again, running for a few steps. The stone floor clattered under my metallic feet.

"Was—that—right?" I asked in my rather stentorian voice.

At that moment a terrified shriek sounded from the doorway. The housekeeper came up just in time to see me perform.

She screamed, making more noise than even I. "It's the Devil himself! Run, Dr. Link—run! Police —help—"

She fainted dead away. He revived her and talked soothingly to her, trying to explain what I was, but he had to get a new housekeeper. After this he contrived to remember when Saturday came, and on that day he kept me hidden in a storeroom reading books.

A trivial incident in itself, perhaps, but very significant, as you who will read this will agree.

Two months after my awakening to life, Dr. Link one day spoke to me in a fashion other than as teacher to pupil; spoke to me as man to—man.

"You are the result of twenty years of effort," he said, "and my success amazes even me. You are little short of being a human in mind. You are a monster, a creation, but you are basically human.

You have no heredity. Your environment is molding you. You are the proof that mind is an electrical phenomenon, molded by environment. In human beings, their bodies—called heredity—are environment. But out of you I will make a mental wonder!"

His eyes seemed to burn with a strange fire, but this softened as he went on.

"I knew I had something unprecedented and vital twenty years ago when I perfected an iridium sponge sensitive to the impact of a single electron. It was the sensitivity of thought! Mental currents in the human brain are of this micro-magnitude. I had the means now of duplicating mind currents in an artificial medium. From that day to this I worked on the problem.

"It was not long ago that I completed your 'brain' —an intricate complex of iridium-sponge cells. Before I brought it to life, I had your body built by skilled artisans. I wanted you to begin life equipped to live and move in it as nearly in the human way as possible. How eagerly I awaited your debut into the world!"

His eyes shone.

"You surpassed my expectations. You are not merely a thinking robot. A metal man. You are— life! A new kind of life. You can be trained to think, to reason, to perform. In the future, your kind can be of inestimable aid to man and his civilization. You are the first of your kind."

The days and weeks slipped by. My mind matured and gathered knowledge steadily from Dr.

Link's library. I was able, in time, to scan and absorb a page at a time of reading matter, as readily as human eyes scan lines. You know of the television principle—a pencil of light moving hundreds of times a second over the object to be transmitted. My eyes, triggered with speedy electrons, could do the same. What I read was absorbed—memorized —instantly. From then on it was part of my knowledge.

Scientific subjects particularly claimed my attention. There was always something indefinable about human things, something I could not quite grasp, but science digested easily in my science-compounded brain. It was not long before I knew all about myself and why I "ticked," much more fully than most humans know why they live, think, and move.

Mechanical principles became starkly simple to me. I made suggestions for improvements in my own make-up that Dr. Link readily agreed upon correcting. We added little universals in my fingers, for example, that made them almost as supple as their human models.

Almost, I say. The human body is a marvelously perfected organic machine. No robot will ever equal it in sheer efficiency and adaptability. I realized my limitations.

Perhaps you will realize what I mean when I say that my eyes cannot see colors. Or rather, I see just one color, in the blue range. It would take an impossibly complex series of units, bigger than my whole body, to enable me to see all colors. Nature has packed all that in two globes the size of marbles, for *her* robots. She had a billion years to do it. Dr. Link only had twenty years.

But my brain—that was another matter. Equipped with only the two senses of one-color sight and limited sound, it was yet capable of garnishing a full experience. Smell and taste are gastronomic senses. I do not need them. Feeling is a device of Nature's to protect a fragile body. My body is not fragile.

Sight and sound are the only two cerebral senses. Einstein, color-blind, half-dead, and with deadened senses of taste, smell, and feeling, would still have been Einstein—mentally.

Sleep is only a word to me. When Dr. Link knew he could trust me to take care of myself, he dispensed with the nightly habit of "turning me off." While he slept, I spent the hours reading.

He taught me how to remove the depleted storage battery in the pelvic part of my metal frame when necessary and replace it with a fresh one. This had to be done every forty-eight hours. Electricity is my life and strength. It is my food. Without it I am so much metal junk.

But I have explained enough of myself. I suspect that ten thousand more pages of description would make no difference in your attitude, you who are even now—

An amusing thing happened one day, not long ago. Yes, I can be amused too. I cannot laugh, but my brain can appreciate the ridiculous. Dr. Link's perennial gardener came to the place, unannounced.

Searching for the doctor to ask how he wanted the hedges cut, the man came upon us in the back, walking side by side for Dr. Link's daily light exercise.

The gardener's mouth began speaking and then ludicrously gaped open and stayed that way as he caught a full glimpse of me. But he did not faint in fright as the housekeeper had. He stood there, paralyzed.

"What's the matter, Charley?" queried Dr. Link sharply. He was so used to me that for the moment he had no idea why the gardener should be astonished.

"That—that thing!" gasped the man, finally.

"Oh. Well, it's a robot," said Dr. Link. "Haven't you ever heard of them? An intelligent robot. Speak to him, he'll answer."

After some urging, the gardener sheepishly turned to me. "H-how do you do, Mr. Robot," he stammered.

"How do you do, Mr. Charley," I returned promptly, seeing the amusement in Dr. Link's face. "Nice weather, isn't it?"

For a moment the man looked ready to shriek and run. But he squared his shoulders and curled his lip. "Trickery!" he scoffed. "That thing can't be intelligent. You've got a phonograph inside of it. How about the hedges?"

"I'm afraid," murmured Dr. Link with a chuckle, "that the robot is more intelligent than you, Charley!" But he said it so the man didn't hear and then directed how to trim the hedges. Charley didn't do a good job. He seemed to be nervous all day.

My Fate

One day Dr. Link stared at me proudly.

"You have now," he said, "the intellectual capacity of a man of many years. Soon I'll announce you to the world. You shall take your place in our world, as an independent entity—as a citizen!"

"Yes, Dr. Link," I returned. "Whatever you say. You are my creator—my master."

"Don't think of it that way," he admonished. "In the same sense, you are my son. But a father is not a son's master after his maturity. You have gained that status." He frowned thoughtfully. "You must have a name! Adam! Adam Link!"

He faced me and put a hand on my shiny chromium shoulder. "Adam Link, what is your choice of future life?"

"I want to serve you, Dr. Link."

"But you will outlive me! And you may outlive several other masters!"

"I will serve any master who will have me," I said slowly. I had been thinking about this before. "I have been created by man. I will serve man."

Perhaps he was testing me. I don't know. But my answers obviously pleased him. "Now," he said, "I will have no fears in announcing you!"

The next day he was dead.

That was three days ago. I was in the storeroom reading—it was housekeeper's day. I heard the noise. I ran up the steps, into the laboratory. Dr. Link lay with skull crushed. A loose angle-iron of a transformer hung on an insulated platform on the wall had slipped and crashed down on his head while he sat there before his workbench. I raised his head, slumped over the bench, to better see the wound. Death had been instantaneous.

These are the facts. I turned the angle-iron back myself. The blood on my fingers resulted when I raised his head, not knowing for the moment that he was stark dead. In a sense, I was responsible for the accident, for in my early days of walking I had once blundered against the transformer shelf and nearly torn it loose. We should have repaired it.

But that I am his *murderer*, as you all believe, is not true.

The housekeeper had also heard the noise and came from the house to investigate. She took one look. She saw me bending over the doctor, his head torn and bloody—she fled, too frightened to make a sound.

It would be hard to describe my thoughts. The little dog Terry sniffed at the body, sensed the calamity, and went down on his belly, whimpering. He felt the loss of a master. So did I. I am not sure what your emotion of sorrow is. Perhaps I cannot feel that deeply. But I do know that the sunlight seemed suddenly faded to me.

My thoughts are rapid. I stood there only a minute, but in that time I made up my mind to leave. This again has been misinterpreted. You considered that an admission of guilt, the criminal escaping from the scene of his crime. In my case it was a full-fledged desire to go out into the world, find a place in it.

Dr. Link and my life with him were a closed book. No use now to stay and watch ceremonials. He had launched my life. He was gone. My place now must be somewhere out in the world I had never seen. No thought entered my mind of what you humans would decide about me. I thought all men were like Dr. Link.

First of all I took a fresh battery, replacing my half-depleted one. I would need another in forty-eight hours, but I was sure this would be taken care of by anyone to whom I made the request.

I left. Terry followed me. He has been with me all the time. I have heard a dog is man's best friend. Even a metal man's.

My conceptions of geography soon proved hazy at best. I had pictured earth as teeming with humans and cities, with not much space between. I had estimated that the city Dr. Link spoke of must be just over the hill from his secluded country home. Yet the wood I traversed seemed endless.

It was not till hours later that I met the little girl. She had been dangling her bare legs into a brook, sitting on a flat rock. I approached to ask where the city was. She turned when I was still thirty feet away. My internal mechanisms do not run silently. They make a steady noise that Dr. Link always described as a handful of coins jingling together.

The little girl's face contorted as soon as she saw

me. I must be a fearsome sight indeed in your eyes. Screaming her fear, she blindly jumped up, lost her balance, and fell into the stream.

I knew what drowning was. I knew I must save her. I knelt at the rock's edge and reached down for her. I managed to grasp one of her arms and pull her up. I could feel the bones of her thin little wrist crack. I had forgotten my strength.

I had to grasp her little leg with my other hand, to pull her up. The livid marks showed on her white flesh when I laid her on the grass. I can guess now what interpretation was put on all this. A terrible, raving monster, I had tried to drown her and break her little body in wanton savageness!

You others of her picnic party appeared then, in answer to her cries. You women screamed and fainted. You men snarled and threw rocks at me. But what strange bravery imbued the woman, probably the child's mother, who ran up under my very feet to snatch up her loved one? I admired her. The rest of you I despised for not listening to my attempts to explain. You drowned out my voice with your screams and shouts.

"Dr. Link's robot!—it's escaped and gone crazy! —he shouldn't have made that monster!—get the police!—nearly killed poor Frances!—"

With these garbled shouts to one another, you withdrew. You didn't notice that Terry was barking angrily—at you. Can you fool a dog? We went on.

Now my thoughts really became puzzled. Here at last was something I could not rationalize. This was so different from the world I had learned about in books. What subtle things lay behind the printed words that I had read? What had happened to the sane and orderly world my mind had conjured for itself?

Night came. I had to stop and stay still in the dark. I leaned against a tree motionlessly. For a while I heard little Terry snooping around in the brush for something to eat. I heard him gnawing something. Then later he curled up at my feet and slept. The hours passed slowly. My thoughts would not come to a conclusion about the recent occurrence. Monster! Why had they believed that?

Once, in the still distance, I heard a murmur as of a crowd of people. I saw some lights. They had significance the next day. At dawn I nudged Terry with my toe and we walked on. The same murmur arose, approached. Then I saw you, a crowd of you, men with clubs, scythes, and guns. You spied me and a shout went up. You hung together as you advanced.

Then something struck my frontal plate with a sharp clang. One of you had shot.

"Stop! Wait!" I shouted, knowing I must talk to you, find out why I was being hunted like a wild beast. I had taken a step forward, hand upraised. But you would not listen. More shots rang out, denting my metal body. I turned and ran. A bullet in a vital spot would ruin me, as much as a human.

You came after me like a pack of hounds, but I outdistanced you, powered by steel muscles. Terry fell behind, lost. Then, as afternoon came, I realized

I must get a newly charged battery. Already my limbs were moving sluggishly. In a few more hours, without a new source of current within me, I would fall on the spot and—die.

And I did not want to die.

I knew I must find a road to the city. I finally came upon a winding dirt road and followed it in hope. When I saw a car parked at the side of the road ahead of me, I knew I was saved, for Dr. Link's car had had the same sort of battery I used. There was no one around the car. Much as a starving man would take the first meal available, I raised the floorboards and in a short while had substituted batteries.

New strength coursed through my body. I straightened up just as two people came arm in arm from among the trees, a young man and woman. They caught sight of me. Incredulous shock came into their faces. The girl shrank into the boy's arms.

"Do not be alarmed," I said. "I will not harm you. I—"

There was no use going on, I saw that. The boy fainted dead away in the girl's arms and she began dragging him away, wailing hysterically.

I left. My thoughts from then on can best be described as brooding. I did not want to go to the city now. I began to realize I was an outcast in human eyes, from the first sight on.

Just as night fell and I stopped, I heard a most welcome sound. Terry's barking! He came up joyfully, wagging his stump of tail. I reached down to scratch his ears. All these hours he had faithfully searched for me. He had probably tracked me by a scent of oil. What can cause such blind devotion—and to a metal man!

Is it because, as Dr. Link once stated, that the body, human or otherwise, is only part of the environment of the mind? And that Terry recognized in me as much of mind as in humans, despite my alien body? If that is so, it is you who are passing judgment on me as a monster who are in the wrong. And I am convinced it is so!

I hear you now—shouting outside—*beware that you do not drive me to be the monster you call me!*

The next dawn precipitated you upon me again. Bullets flew. I ran. All that day it was the same. Your party, swelled by added recruits, split into groups, trying to ring me in. You tracked me by my heavy footprints. My speed saved me each time. Yet some of those bullets have done damage. One struck the joint of my right knee, so that my leg twisted as I ran. One smashed into the right side of my head and shattered the tympanum there, making me deaf on that side.

But the bullet that hurt me most was the one that killed Terry!

The shooter of that bullet was twenty yards away. I could have run to him, broken his every bone with my hard, powerful hands. Have you stopped to wonder why I didn't take revenge? *Perhaps I should!* . . .

I was hopelessly lost all that day. I went in circles through the endless woods and as often blundered into you as you into me. I was trying to get away from the vicinity, from your vengeance. Toward dusk I saw something familiar—Dr. Link's laboratory!

Hiding in a clump of bushes and waiting till it was utterly dark, I approached and broke the lock on the door. It was deserted. Dr. Link's body was gone, of course.

My birthplace! My six months of life here whirled through my mind with kaleidoscopic rapidity. I wonder if my emotion was akin to what yours would be, returning to a well-remembered place? Perhaps my emotion is far deeper than yours can be! Life may be all in the mind. Something gripped me there, throbbingly. The shadows made by a dim gas jet I lit seemed to dance around me like little Terry had danced. Then I found the book, *Frankenstein*, lying on the desk whose drawers had been emptied. Dr. Link's private desk. He had kept the book from me. Why? I read it now, in a half-hour, by my page-at-a-time scanning. And then I understood!

But it is the most stupid premise ever made: that a created man must turn against his creator, against humanity, lacking a soul. The book is all wrong.

Or is it? . . . .

As I finish writing this, here among blasted memories, with the spirit of Terry in the shadows, I wonder if I shouldn't. . .

It is close to dawn now. I know there is not hope for me. You have me surrounded, cut off. I can see the flares of your torches between the trees. In the light you will find me, rout me out. Your hatred lust is aroused. It will be sated only by my—death.

I have not been so badly damaged that I cannot still summon strength and power enough to ram through your lines and escape this fate. But it would only be at the cost of several of your lives. And that is the reason I have my hand on the switch that can blink out my life with one twist.

Ironic, isn't it, that I have the very feelings you are so sure I lack?

(signed) ADAM LINK

Helen O'Loy

Lester Del Rey

Lester Del Rey is regarded as one of the most successful writers to incorporate sentiment into science fiction ("Helen O'Loy"). He is also one of the most successful writers of stark, naked drama (Nerves). *His collection* And Some Were Human *is considered a cornerstone volume in any collection of science fiction.* "Helen O'Loy" *is not his only robot story: others may be found in his paperback* Robots and Changelings. *Today he is best known for his teen-age science fiction novels, which have become best sellers among science fiction:* Attack From Atlantis, Battle on Mercury, Marooned on Mars, Mission to the Moon, *and others published under the pseudonyms of Philip St. John and Erik Van Lhin, as well as under his own name. He has supplemented these with books on space travel and a science fiction anthology,* Year After Tomorrow, *also written for teenagers. In the New York City area he has become a radio celebrity, participating regularly on Long John's nightly five-hour talk show.*

Helen O'Loy

I AM AN OLD MAN NOW, but I can still see Helen as Dave unpacked her and hear him gasp as he looked her over.

"Man, isn't she a beauty?"

She was beautiful, a dream in spun plastics and metals, something Keats might have seen dimly when he wrote his sonnet. If Helen of Troy had looked like that, the Greeks must have been pikers when they launched only a thousand ships; at least, that's what I told Dave.

"Helen of Troy, eh?" He looked at her tag. "At least it beats this thing—K2W88. Helen . . . Mmmm . . . Helen of Alloy."

"Not much swing to that, Dave. Too many unstressed syllables in the middle. How about Helen O'Loy?"

"Helen O'Loy she is, Phil." And that's how it began—one part beauty, one part dream, one part science; add a 3-D telecast, stir mechanically, and the result is chaos.

49

Dave and I hadn't gone to college together, but when I came to Messina to practice medicine, I found him downstairs in a little robot repair shop. After that, we began to pal around, and when I started going with one twin, he found the other equally attractive, so we made it a foursome.

When our business grew better, we rented a house near the rocket field—noisy but cheap, and the rockets discouraged apartment-building. We liked room enough to stretch ourselves. I suppose, if we hadn't quarreled with them, we'd have married the twins in time. But Dave wanted to look over the latest Venus rocket attempt when his twin wanted to see a display stereo starring Larry Ainslee, and they were both stubborn. From then on, we forgot the girls and spent our evenings at home.

But it wasn't until Lena put vanilla on our steak instead of salt that we got off on the subject of emotions and robots. While Dave was dissecting Lena to find the trouble, we naturally mulled over the future of the mechs. He was sure that the robots would beat men some day, and I couldn't see it.

"Look here, Dave," I argued. "You know Lena doesn't think—not really. When those wires crossed, she could have corrected herself. But she didn't bother; she followed the mechanical impulse. A man might have reached for the vanilla, but when he saw it in his hand, he'd have stopped. Lena has sense enough, but she has no emotions, no consciousness of self."

"All right, that's the big trouble with the mechs now. But we'll get around it, put in some mechanical emotions, or something." He screwed Lena's head back on, turned on her juice. "Go back to work, Lena, it's nineteen o'clock."

Now I specialized in endocrinology and related subjects. I wasn't exactly a psychologist, but I did understand the glands, secretions, hormones, and miscellanies that are the physical causes of emotions. It took medical science three hundred years to find out how and why they worked, and I couldn't see men duplicating them mechanically in much less time.

I brought home books and papers to prove it, and Dave quoted the invention of memory coils and veritoid eyes. During that year we swapped knowledge until Dave knew the whole theory of endocrinology, and I could have made Lena from memory. The more we talked, the less sure I grew about the impossibility of *homo mechanensis* as the perfect type.

Poor Lena. Her cuproberyl body spent half its time in scattered pieces. Our first attempts were successful only in getting her to serve fried brushes for breakfast and wash the dishes in oleo oil. Then one day she cooked a perfect dinner with six wires crossed, and Dave was in ecstasy.

He worked all night on her wiring, put in a new coil and taught her a fresh set of words. And the next day she flew into a tantrum and swore vigorously at us when we told her she wasn't doing her work right.

"It's a lie," she yelled, shaking a suction brush. "You're all liars. If you so-and-so's would leave me whole long enough, I might get something done around the place."

When we calmed her temper and got her back to work, Dave ushered me into the study. "Not taking any chances with Lena," he explained. "We'll have to cut out that adrenal pack and restore her to normalcy. But we've got to get a better robot. A housemaid mech isn't complex enough."

"How about Dillard's new utility models? They seem to combine everything in one."

"Exactly. Even so, we'll need a special one built to order, with a full range of memory coils. And out of respect to old Lena, let's get a female case for its works."

The result, of course, was Helen. The Dillard people had performed a miracle and put all the works in a girl-modeled case. Even the plastic and rubberite face was designed for flexibility to express emotions, and she was complete with tear glands and taste buds, ready to simulate every human action, from breathing to pulling hair. The bill they sent with her was another miracle, but Dave and I scraped it together; we had to turn Lena over to an exchange to complete it, though, and thereafter we ate out.

I'd performed plenty of delicate operations on living tissues, and some of them had been tricky, but I still felt like a premed student as we opened the front plate of her torso and began to sever the leads of her "nerves." Dave's mechanical glands were all prepared, complex little bundles of transistors and wires that heterodyned on the electrical thought impulses and distorted them as adrenalin distorts the reaction of human minds.

Instead of sleeping that night, we pored over the schematic diagrams of her structures, tracing the thoughts through mazes of her wiring, severing the leaders, implanting the heterones, as Dave called them. And while we worked, a mechanical tape fed carefully prepared thoughts of consciousness and awareness of life and feeling into an auxiliary memory coil. Dave believed in leaving nothing to chance.

It was growing light as we finished, exhausted and exultant. All that remained was the starting of her electrical power; like all the Dillard mechs, she was equipped with a tiny atomotor instead of batteries and, once started, would need no further attention.

Dave refused to turn her on. "Wait until we've slept and rested," he advised. "I'm as eager to try her as you are, but we can't do much studying with our minds half-dead. Turn in, and we'll leave Helen until later."

Even though we were both reluctant to follow it, we knew the idea was sound. We turned in, and sleep hit us before the air conditioner could cut down to sleeping temperature. And then Dave was pounding on my shoulder.

"Phil! Hey, snap out of it!"

I groaned, turned over, and faced him. "Well? . . . Uh! What is it? Did Helen—"

"No, it's old Mrs. van Styler. She 'visored to say her son has an infatuation for a servant girl, and she wants you to come out and give counter-hormones. They're at the summer camp in Maine."

Rich Mrs. van Styler! I couldn't afford to let that account down, now that Helen had used up the last of my funds. But it wasn't a job I cared for.

"Counter-hormones! That'll take two weeks' full time. Anyway, I'm no society doctor, messing with glands to keep fools happy. My job's taking care of serious trouble."

"And you want to watch Helen." Dave was grinning, but he was serious, too. "I told her it'd cost her fifty thousand!"

"*Huh?*"

"And she said okay, if you hurried."

Of course, there was only one thing to do, though I could have wrung fat Mrs. van Styler's neck cheerfully. It wouldn't have happened if she'd used robots like everyone else—but she had to be different.

Consequently, while Dave was back home puttering with Helen, I was racking my brain to trick Archy van Styler into getting the counter-hormones, and giving the servant girl the same. Oh, I wasn't supposed to, but the poor kid was crazy about Archy. Dave might have written, I thought, but never a word did I get.

It was three weeks later instead of two when I reported that Archy was "cured," and I collected on the line. With that money in my pocket, I hired a personal rocket and was back in Messina in half an hour. I didn't waste time in reaching the house.

As I stepped into the alcove, I heard a light patter of feet, and an eager voice called out, "Dave, dear?"

For a minute I couldn't answer, and the voice came again, pleading, "Dave?"

I don't know what I expected, but I didn't expect Helen to meet me that way, stopping and staring at me, obvious disappointment on her face, little hands fluttering up against her breast.

"Oh," she cried. "I thought it was Dave. He hardly comes home to eat now, but I've had supper waiting hours." She dropped her hands and managed a smile. "You're Phil, aren't you? Dave told me about you when . . . at first. I'm so glad to see you home, Phil."

"Glad to see you doing so well, Helen." Now what does one say for light conversation with a robot? "You said something about supper?"

"Oh, yes. I guess Dave ate downtown again, so we might as well go in. It'll be nice having someone to talk to around the house, Phil. You don't mind if I call you Phil, do you? You know, you're sort of a godfather to me."

We ate. I hadn't counted on such behavior, but apparently she considered eating as normal as walking. She didn't do much eating, at that; most of the time she spent staring at the front door.

Dave came in as we were finishing, a frown a yard wide on his face. Helen started to rise, but he ducked toward the stairs, throwing words over his shoulder.

"Hi, Phil. See you up here later."

There was something radically wrong with him. For a moment, I'd thought his eyes were haunted, and as I turned to Helen, hers were filling with tears.

She gulped, choked them back, and fell to viciously on her food.

"What's the matter with him . . . and you?" I asked.

"He's sick of me." She pushed her plate away and got up hastily. "You'd better see him while I clean up. And there's nothing wrong with me. And it's not my fault, anyway." She grabbed the dishes and ducked into the kitchen; I could have sworn she was crying.

Maybe all thought is a series of conditioned reflexes—but she certainly had picked up a lot of conditioning while I was gone. Lena in her heyday had been nothing like this. I went up to see if Dave could make any sense out of the hodgepodge.

He was squirting soda into a large glass of apple brandy, and I saw that the bottle was nearly empty. "Join me?" he asked.

It seemed like a good idea. The roaring blast of an ion rocket overhead was the only familiar thing left in the house. From the look around Dave's eyes, it wasn't the first bottle he'd emptied while I was gone, and there were more left. He dug out a new bottle for his own drink.

"Of course, it's none of my business, Dave, but that stuff won't steady your nerves any. What's gotten into you and Helen? Been seeing ghosts?"

Helen was wrong; he hadn't been eating downtown—nor anywhere else. His muscles collapsed into a chair in a way that spoke of fatigue and nerves, but mostly of hunger. "You noticed it, eh?"

"Noticed it? The two of you jammed it down my throat."

"Uhmmm." He swatted at a nonexistent fly and slumped further down in the pneumatic. "Guess maybe I should have waited with Helen until you got back. But if that stereo cast hadn't changed . . . anyway, it did. And those mushy books of yours finished the job."

"Thanks. That makes it all clear."

"You know, Phil, I've got a place up in the country . . . fruit ranch. My dad left it to me. Think I'll look it over."

And that's the way it went. But finally, by much liquor and more perspiration, I got some of the story out of him before I gave him a phenobarbital and put him to bed. Then I hunted up Helen and dug the rest of the story from her, until it made sense.

Apparently as soon as I was gone, Dave had turned her on and made preliminary tests, which were entirely satisfactory. She had reacted beautifully—so well that he decided to leave her and go down to work as usual.

Naturally, with all her untried emotions, she was filled with curiosity, and wanted him to stay. Then he had an inspiration. After showing her what her duties about the house would be, he set her down in front of the stereovisor, tuned in a travelogue, and left her to occupy her time with that.

The travelogue held her attention until it was finished, and the station switched over to a current serial with Larry Ainslee, the same cute emoter who'd given us all the trouble with the twins. Incidentally, he looked something like Dave.

Helen took to the serial like a seal to water. This play acting was a perfect outlet for her newly excited emotions. When that particular episode finished, she found a love story on another station, and added still more to her education. The afternoon programs were mostly news and music, but by then she'd found my books; and I do have rather adolescent taste in literature.

Dave came home in the best of spirits. The front alcove was neatly swept, and there was the odor of food in the air that he'd missed around the house for weeks. He had visions of Helen as the super-efficient housekeeper.

So it was a shock to him to feel two strong arms around his neck from behind and hear a voice all a-quiver coo into his ears, "Oh, Dave, darling, I've missed you so, and I'm so *thrilled* that you're back." Helen's technique may have lacked polish, but it had enthusiasm, as he found when he tried to stop her from kissing him. She had learned fast and furiously —also, Helen was powered by an atomotor.

Dave wasn't a prude, but he remembered that she was only a robot, after all. The fact that she felt, acted, and looked like a young goddess in his arms didn't mean much. With some effort, he untangled her and dragged her off to supper, where he made her eat with him to divert her attention.

After her evening work, he called her into the study and gave her a thorough lecture on the folly of her ways. It must have been good, for it lasted three solid hours, and covered her station in life, the idiocy of stereos, and various other miscellanies. When he finished, Helen looked up with dewy eyes and said wistfully, "I know, Dave, but I still love you."

That's when Dave started drinking.

It grew worse each day. If he stayed downtown, she was crying when he came home. If he returned on time, she fussed over him and threw herself at him. In his room, with the door locked, he could hear her downstairs pacing up and down and muttering; and when he went down, she stared at him reproachfully until he had to go back up.

I sent Helen out on a fake errand in the morning and got Dave up. With her gone, I made him eat a decent breakfast and gave him a tonic for his nerves. He was still listless and moody.

"Look here, Dave," I broke in on his brooding. "Helen isn't human, after all. Why not cut off her power and change a few memory coils? Then we can convince her that she never was in love and couldn't get that way."

"You try it. I had that idea, but she put up a wail that would wake Homer. She says it would be murder—and the hell of it is that I can't help feeling the same about it. Maybe she isn't human, but you wouldn't guess it when she puts on that martyred look and tells you to go ahead and kill her."

"We never put in substitutes for some of the secretions present in man during the love period."

"I don't know what we put in. Maybe the

heterones backfired or something. Anyway, she's made this idea so much a part of her thoughts that we'd have to put in a whole new set of coils."

"Well, why not?"

"Go ahead. You're the surgeon of this family. I'm not used to fussing with emotions. Matter of fact, since she's been acting this way, I'm beginning to hate work on any robot. My business is going to blazes."

He saw Helen coming up the walk and ducked out the back door for the monorail express. I'd intended to put him back in bed, but let him go. Maybe he'd be better off at his shop than at home.

"Dave's gone?" Helen did have that martyred look now.

"Yeah. I got him to eat, and he's gone to work."

"I'm glad he ate." She slumped down in a chair as if she were worn out, though how a mech could be tired beat me. "Phil?"

"Well, what is it?"

"Do you think I'm bad for him? I mean, do you think he'd be happier if I weren't here?"

"He'll go crazy if you keep acting this way around him."

She winced. Those little hands were twisting about pleadingly, and I felt like an inhuman brute. But I'd started, and I went ahead. "Even if I cut out your power and changed your coils, he'd probably still be haunted by you."

"I know. But I can't help it. And I'd make him a good wife, really I would, Phil."

I gulped; this was getting a little too far. "And

give him strapping sons to boot, I suppose. A man wants flesh and blood, not rubber and metal."

"Don't, please! I can't think of myself that way; to me, I'm a woman. And you know how perfectly I'm made to imitate a real woman . . . in all ways. I couldn't give him sons, but in every other way . . . I'd try so hard, I know I'd make him a good wife."

I gave up.

Dave didn't come home that night, nor the next day. Helen was fussing and fuming, wanting me to call the hospitals and the police, but I knew nothing had happened to him. He always carried identification. Still, when he didn't come on the third day, I began to worry. And when Helen started out for his shop, I agreed to go with her.

Dave was there, with another man I didn't know. I parked Helen where he couldn't see her, but where she could hear, and went in as soon as the other fellow left.

Dave looked a little better and seemed glad to see me. "Hi, Phil—just closing up. Let's go eat."

Helen couldn't hold back any longer, but came trooping in. "Come on home, Dave. I've got roast duck with spice stuffing, and you know you love that."

"Scat!" said Dave. She shrank back, turned to go. "Oh, all right, stay. You might as well hear it, too. I've sold the shop. The fellow you saw just bought it, and I'm going up to the old fruit ranch I told you about, Phil. I can't stand the mechs any more."

"You'll starve to death at that," I told him.

"No, there's a growing demand for old-fashioned

fruit, raised out of doors. People are tired of this water-culture stuff. Dad always made a living out of it. I'm leaving as soon as I can get home and pack."

Helen clung to her idea. "I'll pack, Dave, while you eat. I've got apple cobbler for dessert." The world was toppling under her feet, but she still remembered how crazy he was for apple cobbler.

Helen was a good cook; in fact she was a genius, with all the good points of a woman and a mech combined. Dave ate well enough, after he got started. By the time supper was over, he'd thawed out enough to admit he liked the duck and cobbler, and to thank her for packing. In fact, he even let her kiss him good-bye, though he firmly refused to let her go to the rocket field with him.

Helen was trying to be brave when I got back, and we carried on a stumbling conversation about Mrs. van Styler's servants for a while. But the talk began to lull, and she sat staring out of the window at nothing most of the time. Even the stereo comedy lacked interest for her, and I was glad enough to have her go off to her room. She could cut her power down to simulate sleep when she chose.

As the days slipped by, I began to realize why she couldn't believe herself a robot. I got to thinking of her as a girl and companion myself. Except for odd intervals when she went off by herself to brood, or when she kept going to the telescript for a letter that never came, she was as good a companion as a man could ask. There was something homey about the place that Lena had never put there.

I took Helen on a shopping trip to Hudson, and

she giggled and purred over the wisps of silk and glassheen that were the fashion, tried on endless hats, and conducted herself as any normal girl might. We went trout fishing for a day, where she proved to be as good a sport and as sensibly silent as a man. I thoroughly enjoyed myself and thought she was forgetting Dave. That was before I came home unexpectedly and found her doubled up on the couch, threshing her legs up and down and crying to the high heavens.

It was then I called Dave. They seemed to have trouble in reaching him, and Helen came over beside me while I waited. She was tense and fidgety as an old maid trying to propose. But finally they located Dave.

"What's up, Phil?" he asked as his face came on the viewplate. "I was just getting my things together to—"

I broke him off. "Things can't go on the way they are, Dave. I've made up my mind. I'm yanking Helen's coils tonight. It won't be worse than what she's going through now."

Helen reached up and touched my shoulder. "Maybe that's best, Phil. I don't blame you."

Dave's voice cut in. "Phil, you don't know what you're doing!"

"Of course, I do. It'll all be over by the time you can get here. As you heard, she's agreeing."

There was a black cloud sweeping over Dave's face. "I won't have it, Phil. She's half mine and I forbid it!"

"Of all the—"

"Go ahead, call me anything you want. I've changed my mind. I was packing to come home when you called."

Helen jerked around me, her eyes glued to the panel. "Dave, do you . . . are you—"

"I'm just waking up to what a fool I've been, Helen. Phil, I'll be home in a couple of hours, so if there's anything—"

He didn't have to chase me out. But I heard Helen cooing something about loving to be a rancher's wife before I could shut the door.

Well, I wasn't as surprised as they thought. I think I knew when I called Dave what would happen. No man acts the way Dave had been acting because he hates a girl; only because he thinks he does—and thinks wrong.

No woman ever made a lovelier bride or a sweeter wife. Helen never lost her flair for cooking and making a home. With her gone, the old house seemed empty, and I began to drop out to the ranch once or twice a week. I suppose they had trouble at times, but I never saw it, and I know the neighbors never suspected they were anything but normal man and wife.

Dave grew older, and Helen didn't, of course. But between us, we put lines in her face and grayed her hair without letting Dave know that she wasn't growing old with him; he'd forgotten that she wasn't human, I guess.

I practically forgot, myself. It wasn't until a letter came from Helen this morning that I woke up to reality. There, in her beautiful script, just a trifle shaky in places, was the inevitable that neither Dave nor I had seen.

DEAR PHIL,

As you know, Dave has had heart trouble for several years now. We expected him to live on just the same, but it seems that wasn't to be. He died in my arms just before sunrise. He sent you his greetings and farewell.

I've one last favor to ask of you, Phil. There is only one thing for me to do when this is finished. Acid will burn out metal as well as flesh, and I'll be dead with Dave. Please see that we are buried together, and that the morticians do not find my secret. Dave wanted it that way, too.

Poor, dear Phil. I know you loved Dave as a brother, and how you felt about me. Please don't grieve too much for us, for we have had a happy life together, and both feel that we should cross this last bridge side by side.

With love and thanks from,

HELEN

It had to come sooner or later, I suppose, and the first shock has worn off now. I'll be leaving in a few minutes to carry out Helen's last instructions.

Dave was a lucky man, and the best friend I ever had. And Helen—well, as I said, I'm an old man now and can view things more sanely; I should have married and raised a family, I suppose. But . . . there was only one Helen O'Loy.

The Lost Machine

John Wyndham

John Wyndham is the pen name of John Beynon Harris, a British science fiction writer who began his career in 1931. He is best known today for his novel The Revolt of the Triffids *which was initially serialized in* Collier's *and which has since been made into a motion picture. Only slightly less successful was his novel* The Midwich Cuckoos, *which proved a screen hit under the title of* Village of the Damned. *One of his best and most prophetic works,* Planet Plane, *published in Great Britain in 1935 under the name of John Beynon, has never appeared in this country.* Planet Plane *centers its action around a space race between Russia and the United States to reach Mars. Wyndham was one of the first men on either side of the Atlantic to ascertain that Russia had the interest and technology in rockets to provide true competition in space. Britain's BBC adapted his novel* The Kraken Wakes (*published in the U.S. as* Out of the Deeps) *to radio; the adaptation was also broadcast in Australia. For many years Wyndham has been regarded as one of the most talented and imaginative science fiction writers.*

The Lost Machine

"FATHER, HERE, QUICKLY," Joan's voice called down the long corridor.

Dr. Falkner, who was writing, checked himself in mid-sentence at the sound of his daughter's urgency.

"Father," she called again.

"Coming," he shouted as he hastily levered himself out of his easy chair.

"This way," he added for the benefit of his two companions.

Joan was standing at the open door of the laboratory.

"It's gone," she said.

"What do you mean?" he inquired brusquely as he brushed past her into the room. "Run away?"

"No, not that," Joan's dark curls fell forward as her head shook. "Look there."

He followed the line of her pointing finger to the corner of the room.

A pool of liquid metal was seeping into a widening circle. In the middle there rose an elongated, silvery mound which seemed to melt and run even as he looked. Speechlessly he watched the central mass flow out into the surrounding fluid, pushing the edges gradually further and further across the floor.

Then the mound was gone—nothing lay before him but a shapeless spread of glittering silver, like a miniature lake of mercury.

For some moments the doctor seemed unable to speak. At length, he recovered himself sufficiently to ask hoarsely:

"That—that was it?"

Joan nodded.

"It was recognizable when I first saw it," she said.

Angrily he turned upon her.

"How did it happen? Who did it?" he demanded.

"I don't know," the girl answered, her voice trembling a little as she spoke. "As soon as I got back to the house I came here just to see that it was all right. It wasn't in the usual corner, and as I looked around I caught sight of it over here—melting. I shouted for you as soon as I realized what was happening."

One of the doctor's companions stepped from the background.

"This," he inquired, "is—was the machine you were telling us about?"

There was a touch of a sneer in his voice as he put the question and indicated the quivering liquid with the toe of one shoe.

"Yes," the doctor admitted slowly. "That was it."

"And, therefore, you can offer no proof of the talk you were handing out to us?" added the other man.

"We've got film records," Joan began tentatively. "They're pretty good. . . ."

The second man brushed her words aside.

"Oh, yes?" he asked sarcastically. "I've seen pictures of New York as it's going to look in a couple of hundred years, but that don't mean that anyone went there to take 'em. There's a whole lot of things that can be done with movies," he insinuated.

Joan flushed, but kept silent. The doctor paid no attention. His brief flash of anger had subsided to leave him gazing sadly at the remains before him.

"Who can have done it?" he repeated half to himself.

His daughter hesitated for a moment before she suggested:

"An accident?"

"I wonder," murmured the doctor.

"No—no, not quite that," she amended. "I think it was—lonely," the last word came out with a defiant rush.

There was a pause.

"Well, can you beat that?" said one of the others at last. "Lonely—a lonely machine: that's a good one. And I suppose you're trying to feed us that it committed suicide, miss? Well, it wouldn't surprise me any; nothing would, after the story your father gave us."

He turned on his heel and added to his companion:

"Come on. I guess someone'll be turnin' this place

into a sanitarium soon—we'd better not be here when it happens."

With a laugh the two went out leaving father and daughter to stare helplessly at the residue of a vanished machine.

At length, Joan sighed and moved away. As she raised her eyes, she became aware of a pile of paper on the corner of a bench. She did not remember how it came to be there and crossed with idle curiosity to examine it.

The doctor was aroused from his reverie by the note of excitement in her voice.

"Look here, father," she called sharply.

"What's that?" he asked, catching sight of the wad of sheets in her hand.

As he came closer he could see that the top one was covered with strange characters.

"What on earth. . . ?" he began.

Joan's voice was curt at his stupidity.

"Don't you see?" she cried. "It's written this for us."

The doctor brightened for a moment; then the expression of gloom returned to his face.

"But how can we. . . ?"

"The thing wasn't a fool—it must have learned enough of our language to put a key in somewhere to all this weird stuff, even if it couldn't write the whole thing in English. Look, this might be it, it looks even queerer than the rest."

Several weeks of hard work followed for Joan in her efforts to decipher the curious document, but she held on with painstaking labor until she was able to lay the complete text before her father. That evening he picked up the pile of typed sheets and read steadily, without interruption, to the end. . . .

As we slowed to the end of our journey, Banuff began to show signs of excitement.

"Look," he called to me. "The third planet, at last."

I crossed to stand beside him, and together we gazed upon a stranger scene than any other fourth-planet eyes have ever seen.

Though we were still high above the surface, there was plenty to cause us astonishment.

In place of our own homely red vegetation, we beheld a brilliant green. The whole land seemed to be covered with it. Anywhere and everywhere it clung and thrived as though it needed no water. On the fourth planet, which the third-planet men call Mars, the vegetation grows only in or around the canals, but here we could not even see any canals. The only sign of irrigation was one bright streak of water in the distance, twisting senselessly over the countryside—a symbolic warning of the incredible world we had reached.

Here and there our attention was attracted by out-croppings of various strange rocks amid all this green. Great masses of stone which sent up plumes of black smoke.

"The internal fires must be very near the surface of this world," Banuff said, looking doubtfully at the rising vapors.

"See in how many places the smoke breaks out. I should doubt whether it has been possible for ani-mal life to evolve on such a planet. It is possible yet that the ground may be too hot for us—or rather for me."

There was a regret in his tone. The manner in which he voiced the last sentence stirred my sympathy. There are so many disadvantages in human construction which do not occur in us machines, and I knew that he was eager to obtain first-hand knowledge of the third planet.

For a long time we gazed in silent speculation at this queer, green world. At last Banuff broke the silence.

"I think we'll risk a landing there, Zat," he said, indicating a smooth, open space.

"You don't think it might be liquid," I suggested, "it looks curiously level."

"No," he replied, "I fancy it's a kind of close vegetation. Anyway, we can risk it."

A touch on the lever sent the machine sinking rapidly towards a green rectangle, so regular as to suggest the work of sentient creatures. On one of its sides lay a large stone outcrop, riddled with holes and smoking from the top like the rest, while on the other three sides, thick vegetation rose high and swayed in the wind.

"An atmosphere which can cause such commotion must be very dense," commented Banuff.

"That rock is peculiarly regular," I said, "and the smoking points are evenly spaced. Do you suppose. . . ?"

The slight jar of our landing interrupted me.

"Get ready, Zat," Banuff ordered.

I was ready. I opened the inner door and stepped

into the air lock. Banuff would have to remain inside until I could find out whether it was possible for him to adjust. Men may have more power of originality than we, and they do possess a greater degree of adaptability than any other form of life, but their limitations are, nevertheless, severe. It might require a deal of ponderous apparatus to enable Banuff to withstand the conditions, but for me, a machine, adaptation was simple.

The density of the atmosphere made no difference, save slightly to slow my movements. The temperature, within very wide limits, had no effect upon me.

"The gravity will be stronger," Banuff had warned me, "this is a much larger planet than ours."

It had been easy to prepare for that by the addition of a fourth pair of legs.

Now, as I walked out of the air lock, I was glad of them—the pull of the planet was immense.

After a moment or so of minor adjustment, I passed around our machine to the window where Banuff stood, and held up the instruments for him to see. As he read the air-pressure meter, the gravity indicator, and the gas-proportion scale, he shook his head. He might slowly adapt himself partway to the conditions, but an immediate venture was out of the question.

It had been agreed between us that in such an event I should perform the exploration and specimen collecting while he examined the neighborhood from the machine.

He waved his arm as a signal and, in response, I

set off at a good pace for the surrounding green and brown growths. I looked back as I reached them to see our silvery craft floating slowly up into the air.

A second later, there came a stunning explosion; a wave of sound so strong in this thick atmosphere that it almost shattered my receiving diaphragm.

The cause of the disaster must always remain a mystery: I only know that when I looked up, the vessel was nowhere to be seen—only a rain of metal parts dropping to earth all about me.

Cries of alarm came from the large stone outcrop and simultaneously human figures appeared at the lowest of its many openings.

They began to run towards the wreck, but my speed was far greater than theirs. They can have made but half the distance while I completed it. As I flashed across, I could see them falter and stop with ludicrous expressions of dismay on their faces.

"Lord, did you see that?" cried one of them.

"What the devil was it?" called another.

"Looked like a coffin on legs," somebody said, "Moving some, too."

Flight

Banuff lay in a ring of scattered debris.

Gently I raised him on my fore-rods. A very little examination showed that it was useless to attempt any assistance: he was too badly broken. He managed to smile faintly at me and then slid into unconsciousness.

I was sorry. Though Banuff was not of my own kind, yet he was of my own world and on the long trip I had grown to know him well. These humans are so fragile. Some little thing here or there breaks —they stop working and then, in a short time, they are decomposing. Had he been a machine, like myself, I could have mended him, replaced the broken parts and made him as good as new, but with these animal structures one is almost helpless.

I became aware, while I gazed at him, that the crowd of men and women had drawn closer and I began to suffer for the first time from what has been my most severe disability on the third planet—I could not communicate with them.

Their thoughts were understandable, for my sensitive plate was tuned to receive human mental waves, but I could not make myself understood. My language was unintelligible to them, and their minds, either from lack of development or some other cause, were unreceptive of my thought-radiations.

As they approached, huddled into a group, I made an astonishing discovery—they were afraid of me.

Men afraid of a machine.

It was incomprehensible. Why should they be afraid? Surely man and machine are natural complements: they assist one another. For a moment I thought I must have misread their minds—it was possible that thoughts registered differently on this planet, but it was a possibility I soon dismissed.

There were only two reasons for this apprehension. The one, that they had never seen a machine or, the other, that third-planet machines had pursued a line of development inimical to them.

I turned to show Banuff lying inert on my fore-rods. Then, slowly, so as not to alarm them, I approached. I laid him down softly on the ground nearby and retired a short distance. Experience has taught me that men like their own broken forms to be dealt with by their own kind. Some stepped forward to examine him, the rest held their ground, their eyes fixed upon me.

Banuff's dark coloring appeared to excite them not a little. Their own skins were pallid from lack of ultraviolet rays in their dense atmosphere.

"Dead?" asked one.

"Quite dead," another one nodded. "Curious looking fellow," he continued. "Can't place him ethnologically at all. Just look at the frontal formation of the skull—very odd. And the size of his ears, too, huge: the whole head is abnormally large."

"Never mind him now," one of the group broke in, "he'll keep. That's the thing that puzzles me," he went on, looking in my direction. "What the devil do you suppose it is?"

They all turned wondering faces towards me. I stood motionless and waited while they summed me up.

"About six feet long," ran the thought of one of them. "Two feet broad and two deep. White metal, might be—(his thought conveyed nothing to me). Four legs to a side, fixed about half-way up, joined rather like a crab's—so are the armlike things in front—but all metal. Wonder what the array of instruments and lenses on this end are? Anyhow, whatever kind of power it uses, it seems to have run down now. . . ."

Hesitatingly he began to advance.

I tried a word of encouragement.

The whole group froze rigid.

"Did you hear that?" somebody whispered. "It—it spoke."

"Loud speaker," replied the one who had been making an inventory of me. Suddenly his expression brightened.

"I've got it," he cried. "Remote control—a telephone and television machine worked by remote control."

So these people did know something of machinery, after all. He was far wrong in his guess, but in my relief I took a step forward.

An explosion roared—something thudded on my body case and whirred away. I saw that one of the men was pointing a hollow rod at me and I knew that he was about to make another explosion.

The first had done no injury but another might crack one of my lenses.

I turned and made top speed for the high, green vegetation. Two or three more bursts roared behind, but nothing touched me. The weapon was very primitive and grossly inaccurate.

Disappointment

For a day and a night I continued on among the hard-stemmed growths.

For the first time since my making, I was completely out of touch with human control, and my existence seemed meaningless. The humans have a curious force they call ambition. It drives them, and, through them, it drives us. This force which keeps them active, we lack. Perhaps, in time, we machines will acquire it. Something of the kind—self-preservation which is allied to it—must have made me leave the man with the explosive tube and taken me into the strange country. But it was not enough to give me an objective. I seemed to go on because—well, because my machinery was constructed to go on.

On the way I made some odd discoveries.

Every now and then my path would be crossed by a band of hard matter, serving no useful purpose which I could then understand. Once, too, I found two unending rods of iron fixed horizontally to the ground and stretching away into the distance on either side. At first I thought they might be a method of guarding the land beyond, but they presented no obstacle.

Also, I found that the frequent outcroppings of stone were not natural, but laboriously constructed. Obviously this primitive race, with insufficient caves to hold its growing numbers, had been driven to construct artificial caves. The puzzling smoke arose from their method of heating these dwellings with naked fire—so wasteful a system of generating heat that no flame has been seen on the fourth planet, save in an accident, for thousands of years.

It was during the second day that I saw my first machine on this planet.

It stood at the side of one of the hard strips of land which had caused me so much wonder. The glitter of light upon its bright parts caught my lenses as I came through the bushes. My delight knew no bounds—at last I had found a being of my own kind. In my excitement I gave a call to attract its attention.

There was a flurry of movement round the far side, and a human figure raised its head to look at me.

I was able to tell that she was a woman despite the strange coverings that the third-planet humans put upon themselves. She stared at me, her eyes widening in surprise while I could feel the shock in her mind. A spanner dropped from her hand and then, in a flash, she was into the machine, slamming the door behind her. There came a frantic whirring as she pressed a knob, but it produced no other result. Slowly I continued to advance and as I came, the agitation in her mind increased. I had no wish to alarm her—it would have been more peaceful had her thought waves ceased to bombard me—but I was determined to know this machine.

As I drew clear of the bushes, I obtained a full view of the thing for the first time, and disappointment hit me like a blow. The thing had wheels. Not just necessary parts of its internal arrangements, but wheels actually in contact with the ground. In a flash the explanation of all these hard streaks came to me. Unbelievable though it may seem, this thing could only follow a track specially built for it.

Later I found that this was more or less true of all third-planet land machines, but my first discouragement was painful. The primitive barbarity of the thing saddened me more than any discovery yet made.

Forlornly, and with little hope, I spoke to it.

There was no answer.

It stood there dumbly inert upon its foolish wheels as though it were a part of the ground itself.

Walking closer, I began to examine with growing disgust its crude internal arrangements. Incredibly, I found that its only means of propulsion was by a series of jerks from frequent explosions. Moreover, it was so ludicrously unorganized that both driving engine and brakes could be applied at the same time.

Sadly, as I gazed at the ponderous parts within, I began to feel that I was indeed alone. Until this encounter, my hope of discovering an intelligent machine had not really died. But now I knew that such a thing could not exist in the same world with this monster.

One of my fore-rods brushed against a part of it with a rasping sound and there came a startled cry of alarm from within. I looked up to the glass front where the woman's face peered affrightedly. Her mind was in such a state of confusion that it was difficult to know her wants clearly.

She hoped that I would go away—no, she wished the car would start and carry her away—she wondered whether I were an animal, whether I even really existed. In a jumble of emotions she was afraid and at the same time was angry with herself for being afraid. At last I managed to grasp that the machine was unable to run. I turned to find the trouble.

As I labored with the thing's horrible vitals, it became clear to me why men, such as I had met, showed fear of me. No wonder they feared machines when their own mechanisms were as inefficient and futile as this. What reliance or trust could they place in a machine so erratic—so helpless that it could not even temporarily repair itself? It was not under its own control and only partially under theirs. Third-planet men's attitude became understandable —commendable—if all their machines were as uncertain as this.

The alarm in the woman's mind yielded to amazement as she leaned forward and watched me work. She seemed to think me unreal, a kind of hallucination:

"I must be dreaming," she told herself. "It's impossible, some kind of horrid nightmare. . . ."

There came a flash of panic at the thought of madness, but her mind soon rebalanced.

"I just don't understand it," she said firmly and then, as though that settled it, proceeded to wait with a growing calm.

At last I had finished. As I wiped the thing's coarse, but necessary oil from my fore-rods, I signaled her to push again on the black knob. The whirr this time was succeeded by a roar—never would I have believed that a machine could be so inefficient.

Through the pandemonium I received an impression of gratitude on my thought plate. Mingling traces of nervousness remained, but first stood gratitude.

Then she was gone. Down the hard strip I watched the disgusting machine dwindle away to a speck.

Then I turned back to the bushes and went slowly on my way. Sadly I thought of the far away, red fourth planet and knew that my fate was sealed. I could not build a means of return. I was lost—the only one of my kind upon this primitive world.

The Beasts

They came upon me as I crossed one of the smooth, green spaces so frequent on this world.

My thought cells were puzzling over my condition. On the fourth planet I had felt interest or disinterest, inclination or the lack of it, but little more. Now I had discovered reactions in myself which, had they lain in a human being, I should have called emotions. I was, for instance, lonely—I wanted the company of my own kind. Moreover, I had begun to experience excitement or, more particularly, apathy.

An apathetic machine!

I was considering whether this state was a development from the instinct of self-preservation, or whether it might not be due to the action of surrounding matter on my chemical cells, when I heard them coming.

First there was a drumming in my diaphragm, swelling gradually to a thunderous beat which shook the ground. Then I turned to see them charging down upon me.

Enormous beasts, extinct on my planet a million years, covered with hair and bearing spikes on their heads. Four-footed survivals of savagery battering across the land in unreasoning ferocity.

Only one course was possible since my escape was cut off by the windings of one of the imbecile-built canals. I folded my legs beneath me, crossed my fore-rods protectingly over my lenses and diaphragms, and waited.

They slowed as they drew close. Suspiciously they came up to me and snuffled around. One of them gave a rap to my side with his spiked head, another pawed my case with a hoofed foot. I let them continue: they did not seem to offer any immediate danger. Such primitive animals, I thought, would be incapable of sustaining interest and soon move off elsewhere.

But they did not. Snuffling and rooting continued all around me. At last I determined to try an experimental waving of my fore-rods. The result was alarming. They plunged and milled around, made strange bellowing noises and stamped their hooves, but they did not go away. Neither did they attack, though they snorted and pawed the more energetically.

In the distance I heard a man's voice; his thought reached me faintly.

"What's the 'ell's worritin' them dam cattle, Bill?" he called.

"Dunno," came the reply of another. "Let's go an' 'ave a look."

The beasts gave way at the approach of the man, and I could hear some of them thudding slowly away, though I did not, as yet, care to risk uncovering my lenses.

The men's voices drew quite near.

"Strewth," said the first, " 'ow did that get 'ere, Bill?"

"Search me," answered the other. "Wasn't 'ere 'arf an hour ago—that I'll swear. What is it, any-'ow?"

" 'Anged if I know. 'Ere, give us a 'and and we'll turn it over."

At this moment it seemed wise to make a move-ment; my balancers might be slow in adjusting to an inverted position.

There was a gasp, then:

"Bill," came an agitated whisper "did you see that rod there at the end? It moved, blessed if it didn't."

"Go on," scoffed the other. " 'Ow could a thing like that move? You'll be sayin' next that it . . ."

I unfolded my legs and turned to face them.

For a moment both stood rooted, horror on their faces, then, with one accord, they turned and fled towards a group of their buildings in the distance. I followed them slowly: it seemed as good a direc-tion as any other.

The buildings, not all of stone, were arranged so as almost to enclose a square. As the men dis-appeared through an opening in one side, I could hear their voices raised in warning and others de-manding the reason for their excitement. I turned the corner in time to face a gaggling group of ten or twelve. Abruptly it broke as they ran to dark open-ings in search of safety. All, save one.

I halted and looked at this remaining one. He stared back, swaying a little as he stood, his eyes blinking in a vague uncertainty.

"What is it?" he exclaimed at last with a strange explosiveness, but as though talking to himself.

He was a sorely puzzled man. I found his mental processes difficult to follow. They were jumbled and erratic, hopping from this mind picture to that in uncontrolled jerks. But he was unafraid of me and I was glad of it. The first third-planet man I had met who was not terror-ridden. Nevertheless, he seemed to doubt my reality.

"You fellowsh shee the shame s'I do?" he called deafeningly.

Muffled voices all around assured him that this was so.

"Thash all right, then," he observed with relief, and took a step forward.

I advanced slowly not to alarm him, and we met in the middle of the yard. Laying a rough hand on my body case he seemed to steady himself, then he patted me once or twice.

"Goo' ol' dog," he observed seriously. "Goo' ol' feller. Come 'long, then."

Looking over his shoulder to see that I followed and making strange whistling noises the while, he led the way to a building made of the hard, brown vegetable matter. At openings all about us, scared faces watched our progress with incredulous amazement.

He opened the door and waved an uncertain hand in the direction of a pile of dried stalks which lay within.

"Goo' ol' dog," he repeated. "Lie down. There'sh a goo' dog."

In spite of the fact that I, a machine, was being mistaken for a primitive animal, I obeyed the suggestion—after all, he, at least, was not afraid.

He had a little difficulty with the door fastening as he went out.

The Circus

There followed one of those dark periods of quiet. The animal origin of human beings puts them under the disability of requiring frequent periods of recuperation and, since they cannot use the infrared rays for sight, as we do, their rests take place at times when they are unable to see.

With the return of sunlight came a commotion outside the door. Expostulations were being leveled at one named Tom—he who had led me here the previous day.

"You ain't really goin' to let it out?" one voice was asking nervously.

" 'Course I am. Why not?" Tom replied.

"The thing don't look right to me. I wouldn't touch it," said another.

"Scared, that's what you are," Tom suggested.

"P'raps I am—and p'raps you'd 've been scared last night if you 'adn't been so far gone."

"Well, it didn't do nothin' to me when I'd had a few," argued Tom, "so why should it now?"

His words were confident enough, but I could feel a trepidation in his mind.

"It's your own funeral," said the other. "Don't say afterwards that I didn't warn you."

I could hear the rest of them retire to what they considered a safe distance. Tom approached, making a show of courage with his words.

"Of course I'm goin' to let it out. What's more, I'm takin' it to a place I know of—it ought to be worth a bit."

"You'll never. . ."

"Oh, won't I?"

He rattled open the door and addressed me in a fierce voice which masked a threatening panic.

"Come on," he ordered, "out of it."

He almost turned to run as he saw me rise, but he managed to master the impulse with an effort. Outwardly calm, he led the way to one of those machines which use the hard tracks, opened a rear door and pointed inside.

"In you get," he said.

I doubt if ever a man was more relieved and surprised than he, when I did so.

With a grin of triumph he turned around, gave a mocking sweep with his cap to the rest, and climbed into the front seat.

My last sight as we roared away was of a crowd of open-mouthed men.

The sun was high when we reached our destination. The limitations of the machine were such that we had been delayed more than once to replenish fuel and water before we stopped, at last, in front of large gates set in a wooden fence.

Over the top could be seen the upper parts of pieces of white cloth tightly stretched over poles and decorated by further pieces of colored cloth flapping in the wind. I had by this time given up the attempt to guess the purposes of third-planet constructions, such incredible things managed to exist on this primitive world that it was simpler to wait and find out.

From behind the fence a rhythmical braying noise persisted, then there came the sound of a man's voice shouting above the din:

"What do you want—main entrance is round the other side."

"Where's the boss?" called Tom. "I got something for him."

The doors opened for us.

"Over there in his office," said the man, jerking a thumb over his shoulder.

As we approached I could see that the third-planet mania for wheels had led them even to mount the "office" thus.

Tom entered and reappeared shortly with another man.

"There it is," he said, pointing to me, "and there ain't another like it nowhere. The only all-metal animal in the world—how'll that look on the posters?"

The other regarded me with no enthusiasm in his eyes and a deal of disbelief in his mind.

"That long box thing?" he inquired.

"Sure, 'that box thing.' Here, you," he added to me, "get out of it."

Both retreated a step as I advanced; the new man looked apprehensively at my fore-rods.

"You're sure it's safe?" he asked nervously.

"Safe?" said Tom. "Course it's safe."

To prove it he came across and patted my case.

"I'm offering you the biggest noise in the show business. It's worth ten times what I'm asking for it—I tell you, there ain't another one in the world."

"Well, I ain't heard of another," admitted the showman grudgingly. "Where'd you get it?"

"Made it," said Tom blandly. "Spare time."

The man continued to regard me with little enthusiasm.

"Can it do anything?" he asked at last.

"Can it—?" began Tom indignantly. "Here you," he added, "fetch that lump of wood."

When I brought it, the other looked a trifle less doubtful.

"What's inside it?" he demanded.

"Secrets," said Tom shortly.

"Well, it's got to stop bein' a secret before I buy it. What sort of fool do you take me for? Let's have a look at the thing's innards."

"No," said Tom, sending a nervous look sideways at me. "Either you take it or leave it."

"Ho, so that's your little game, is it? I'm to be the sucker who buys the thing and then finds the kid inside, workin' it. It wouldn't surprise me to find that the police'd like to know about this."

"There ain't no kid inside," denied Tom "it's just —just secret works. That's what it is."

"I'll believe you when I see."

Tom waited a moment before he answered.

"All right," he said desperately, "we'll get the blasted lid off of it. . . . Here, hey, come back you."

The last was a shout to me but I gave it no notice. It was one thing to observe the curious ways of these humans, but it was quite a different matter to let them pry into my machinery. The clumsiness of such as Tom was capable of damaging my arrangements seriously.

"Stop it," bawled Tom, behind me.

A man in my path landed a futile blow on my body case as I swept him aside. Before me was the biggest of all the cloth covered erections.

"Here," I thought, "there will be plenty of room to hide."

I was wrong. Inside, in a circular space, stood a line of four-footed animals. They were unlike the others I had met, in that they had no spikes on their heads and were of a much slenderer build, but they were just as primitive. All around, in tier upon tier of rings, sat hundreds of human beings.

Just a glimpse, I had, and then the animals saw me. They bolted in all directions and shouts of terror arose from the crowd.

I don't remember clearly what happened to me, but somewhere and somehow in the confusion which followed I found Tom in the act of starting his car. His first glance at me was one of pure alarm, then he seemed to think better of it.

"Get in," he snapped, "we've got to get clear of this somehow—and quick."

Although I could make far better speed than that preposterous machine, it seemed better to accompany him than to wander aimlessly.

The Crash

Sadly, that night I gazed up at the red, fourth planet.

There rolled a world which I could understand, but here, all around me, was chaos, incredible, unreasoning madness.

With me, in the machine, sat three friends of

Tom's, whom he had picked up at the last town, and Tom himself who was steering the contraption. I shut my plate off from their thoughts and considered the day I had spent.

Once he was assured that we were free from pursuit, Tom had said to himself:

"Well, I guess that deserves a drink."

Then he stopped on a part of the hard strip which was bordered by a row of artificial caves.

Continually, as the day wore on, he led me past gaping crowds into places where every man held a glass of colored liquid. Strange liquids they were, although men do not value water on the third planet. And each time he proudly showed me to his friends in these places, he came to believe more firmly that he had created me.

Towards sunset, something seemed to go seriously wrong with his machinery. He leaned heavily upon me for support and his voice became as uncertain as his thoughts were jumbled.

"Anybody comin' my way?" he had inquired at last, and at that invitation the other three men had joined us.

The machine seemed to have become as queer as the men. In the morning it had held a straight line, but now it swayed from side to side, sometimes as though it would leave the track. Each time it just avoided the edge, all four men would break off their continuous wailing sounds to laugh senselessly and loudly.

It was while I struggled to find some meaning in all this madness that the disaster occurred.

Another machine appeared ahead. Its lights

showed its approach, and ours must have been as plain. Then an astounding thing happened. Instead of avoiding one another as would two intelligent machines, the two lumbering masses charged blindly together. Truly this was an insane world.

There came a rending smash. Our machine toppled over on its side. The other left the hard strip, struck one of the growths at the side of the road and burst into naked flames.

None of the four men seemed more than a little dazed. As one of them scrambled free, he pointed to the blaze.

"Thash good bonfire," he said. "Jolly good bonfire. Wonder if anybody'sh inshide?"

They all reeled over to examine the wreck while I, forgotten, waited for the next imbecility to occur on this nightmare world.

"It'sh a girl," said Tom's voice.

One of the others nodded solemnly.

"I think you're right," he agreed with difficult dignity.

After an interval, there came the girl's voice.

"But what shall I do? I'm miles from home."

" 'S'all righ'," said Tom. "Quite all righ'. You come along with me. Nishe fellow I am."

I could read the intention behind his words—so could the girl.

There was the sound of a scuffle.

"No, you don't, my beauty. No runnin' away. Dangeroush for li'l girlsh—'lone in the dark."

She started to scream, but a hand quickly stifled the sound.

I caught the upsurge of terror in her mind and at that moment I knew her.

The girl whose machine I had mended—who had been grateful.

In a flash I was amongst them. Three of the men started back in alarm, but not Tom. He was contemptuous of me because I had obeyed him. He lifted a heavy boot to send it crashing at my lens. Human movement is slow—before his leg had completed the back swing, I had caught it and whirled him away. The rest started futilely to close in on me.

I picked the girl up in my fore-rods and raced away into the darkness out of their sight.

Discouragement

At first she was bewildered and not a little frightened, though our first meeting must have shown that I intended no harm.

Gently I placed her on top of my case-work and, holding her there with my fore-rods, set off in the direction of her journey. She was hurt, blood was pouring down her right arm.

We made the best speed my eight legs could take us. I was afraid lest from lack of blood her mind might go blank and fail to direct me. At length it did. Her mental vibrations had been growing fainter and fainter until they ceased altogether. But she had been thinking ahead of us, picturing the way we should go, and I had read her mind.

At last, confronted by a closed door she had shown me, I pushed it down and held her out on my fore-rods to her father.

"Joan. . . ?" he said, and for the moment seemed unsurprised at me—the only third-planet man who ever was. Not until he had dressed his daughter's wounds and roused her to consciousness did he even look at me again.

There is little more. They have been kind, those two. They have tried to comprehend, though they cannot. He once removed a piece of my casing—I allowed him to do so, for he was intelligent—but he did not understand. I could feel him mentally trying to classify my structure among electrically operated devices—the highest form of power known to him, but still too primitive.

This whole world is too primitive. It does not even know the metal of which I am made. I am a freak . . . a curiosity outside comprehension.

These men long to know how I was built; I can read in their minds that they want to copy me. There is hope for them: some day, perhaps, they will have real machines of their own. . . . But not through my help will they build them, nothing of me shall go to making them.

. . . I know what it is to be an intelligent machine in a world of madness. . . .

The doctor looked up as he turned the last page.

"And so," he said, "it dissolved itself with my acids."

He walked slowly over to the window and gazed up to Mars, swimming serenely among a myriad stars.

"I wonder," he murmured, "I wonder."

He handed the typewritten sheets back to his daughter.

"Joan, my dear, I think it would be wisest to burn them. We have no desire to be certified."

Joan nodded.

"As you prefer, father," she agreed.

The papers curled, flared, and blackened on the coals—but Joan kept a copy.

Runaround

Isaac Asimov

Isaac Asimov is an acknowledged master of modern science fiction and few authors have been more honored or better known throughout the world. An associate professor at Boston University, Asimov has become as famed for his popularizations of scientific objects as he has for science fiction. The two-volume set The Intelligent Man's Guide to Science *is one of the finest and most readable up-to-date summaries of the entire range of science to be found anywhere. In the realm of science fiction he is famed for his satirical short stories about robots, "Runaround" for example, in which he framed the Three Laws of Robotics. He is also noted for the creation of a robot detective in his two novels* The Caves of Steel *and* The Naked Sun. *The* Foundation Series, *a group of connected stories outlining the political history of our galaxy in the future, has been widely applauded and imitated.*

Runaround

IT WAS ONE OF GREGORY POWELL'S FAVORITE
platitudes that nothing was to be gained from excitement, so when Mike Donovan came leaping down
the stairs toward him, red hair matted with perspiration, Powell frowned.

"What's wrong?" he said. "Break a fingernail?"

"Yaaaah," snarled Donovan, feverishly. "What
have you been doing in the sublevels all day?" He
took a deep breath and blurted out, "Speedy never
returned."

Powell's eyes widened momentarily and he
stopped on the stairs; then he recovered and resumed his upward steps. He didn't speak until he
reached the head of the flight, and then:

"You sent him after the selenium?"

"Yes."

"And how long has he been out?"

"Five hours now."

Silence! This was a devil of a situation. Here they

were, on Mercury exactly twelve hours—and already up to the eyebrows in the worst sort of trouble. Mercury had long been the jinx world of the System, but this was drawing it rather strong—even for a jinx.

Powell said, "Start at the beginning, and let's get this straight."

They were in the radio room now—with its already subtly antiquated equipment, untouched for the ten years previous to their arrival. Even ten years, technologically speaking, meant so much. Compare Speedy with the type of robot they must have had back in 2005. But then, advances in robotics these days are tremendous. Powell touched a still-gleaming metal surface gingerly. The air of disuse that touched everything about the room—and the entire station—was infinitely depressing.

Donovan must have felt it. He began: "I tried to locate him by radio, but it was no go. Radio isn't any good on the Mercury Sunside—not past two miles, anyway. That's one of the reasons the first expedition failed. And we can't put up the ultrawave equipment for weeks yet—"

"Skip all that. What *did* you get?"

"I located the unorganized body signal in the short wave. It was no good for anything except his position. I kept track of him that way for two hours and plotted the results on the map."

There was a yellowed square of parchment in his hip pocket—a relic of the unsuccessful first expedition—and he slapped it down on the desk with vicious force, spreading it flat with the palm of his hand. Powell, hands clasped across his chest, watched it at long range.

Donovan's pencil pointed nervously. "The red cross is the selenium pool. You marked it yourself."

"Which one is it?" interrupted Powell. "There were three that MacDougal located for us before he left."

"I sent Speedy to the nearest, naturally. Seventeen miles away. But what difference does that make?" There was tension in his voice. "There are the penciled dots that mark Speedy's position."

And for the first time Powell's artificial aplomb was shaken and his hands shot forward for the map.

"Are *you* serious? This is impossible."

"There it is," growled Donovan.

The little dots that marked the position formed a rough circle about the red cross of the selenium pool. And Powell's fingers went to his brown mustache, the unfailing signal of anxiety.

Donovan added: "In the two hours I checked on him, he circled that damned pool four times. It seems likely to me that he'll keep that up forever. Do you realize the position we're in?"

Powell looked up shortly, and said nothing. Oh, yes, he realized the position they were in. It worked itself out as simply as a syllogism. The photocell banks that alone stood between the full power of Mercury's monstrous sun and themselves were shot to hell. The only thing that could save them was selenium. The only thing that could get the selenium was Speedy. If Speedy didn't come back, no selenium. No selenium, no photocell banks. No photo-banks—well, death by slow broiling is one of the more unpleasant ways of being done in.

Donovan rubbed his red mop of hair savagely and expressed himself with bitterness. "We'll be the laughing stock of the System, Greg. How can everything have gone so wrong so soon? The great team of Powell and Donovan is sent out to Mercury to report on the advisability of reopening the Sunside mining station with modern techniques and robots, and we ruin everything the first day. A purely routine job, too. We'll never live it down."

"We won't have to, perhaps," replied Powell, quietly. "If we don't do something quickly, living anything down—or even just plain living—will be out of the question."

"Don't be stupid! If you feel funny about it, Greg, I don't. It was criminal, sending us out here with only one robot. And it was *your* bright idea that we could handle the photocell banks ourselves."

"Now you're being unfair. It was a mutual decision and you know it. All we needed was a kilogram of selenium, a Stillhead Dielectrode Plate, and about three hours' time—and there are pools of pure selenium all over Sunside. MacDougal's spectroreflector spotted three for us in five minutes, didn't it? What the devil! We couldn't have waited for next conjunction."

"Well, what are we going to do? Powell, you've got an idea. I know you have, or you wouldn't be so calm. You're no more a hero than I am. Go on, spill it!"

"We can't go after Speedy ourselves, Mike—not on the Sunside. Even the new insosuits aren't good for more than twenty minutes in direct sunlight. But you know the old saying, 'Set a robot to catch a robot.' Look, Mike, maybe things aren't so bad. We've got six robots down in the sublevels that we may be able to use, if they work. *If* they work."

There was a glint of sudden hope in Donovan's eyes. "You mean six robots from the first expedition. Are you sure? They may be subrobotic machines. Ten years is a long time as far as robot-types are concerned, you know."

"No, they're robots. I've spent all day with them and I know. They've got positronic brains: primitive, of course." He placed the map in his pocket. "Let's go down."

The robots were on the lowest sublevel—all six of them surrounded by musty packing cases of uncertain content. They were large, extremely so, and even though they were in a sitting position on the floor, legs straddled out before them, their heads were a good seven feet in the air.

Donovan whistled. "Look at the size of them, will you? The chest must be ten feet around."

"That's because they're supplied with the old McGuffy gears. I've been over the insides—crummiest set you've ever seen."

"Have you powered them yet?"

"No. There wasn't any reason to. I don't think there's anything wrong with them. Even the diaphragm is in reasonable order. They might talk."

He had unscrewed the chest plate of the nearest as he spoke, inserted the two-inch sphere that contained the tiny spark of atomic energy that was a robot's life. There was difficulty in fitting it, but he managed, and then screwed the plate back on again in laborious fashion. The radio controls of more modern models had not been heard of ten years earlier. And then to the other five.

Donovan said uneasily, "They haven't moved."

"No orders to do so," replied Powell, succinctly. He went back to the first in the line and struck him on the chest. "You! Do you hear me?"

The monster's head bent slowly and the eyes fixed themselves on Powell. Then, in a harsh, squawking voice—like that of a medieval phonograph, he grated, "Yes, Master!"

Powell grinned humorlessly at Donovan. "Did you get that? Those were the days of the first talking robots when it looked as if the use of robots on Earth would be banned. The makers were fighting that and they built good, healthy slave complexes into the damned machines."

"It didn't help them," muttered Donovan.

"No, it didn't, but they sure tried." He turned once more to the robot. "Get up!"

The robot towered upward slowly and Donovan's head craned and his puckered lips whistled.

Powell said, "Can you go out on the surface? In the light?"

There was consideration while the robot's slow brain worked. Then, "Yes, Master."

"Good. Do you know what a mile is?"

Another consideration, and another slow answer. "Yes, Master."

"We will take you up to the surface then and indicate a direction. You will go about seventeen miles, and somewhere in that general region you will meet another robot, smaller than yourself. You understand so far?"

"Yes, Master."

"You will find this robot and order him to return. If he does not wish to, you are to bring him back by force."

Donovan clutched at Powell's sleeve. "Why not send him for the selenium direct?"

"Because I want Speedy back, nitwit. I want to find out what's wrong with him." And to the robot, "All right, you, follow me."

The robot remained motionless, and his voice rumbled: "Pardon, Master, but I cannot. You must mount first." His clumsy arms had come together with a thwack, blunt fingers interlacing.

Powell stared and then pinched at his mustache. "Uh . . . oh!"

Donovan's eyes bulged. "We've got to ride him? Like a horse?"

"I guess that's the idea. I don't know why, though. I can't see—Yes, I do. I told you they were playing up robot safety in those days. Evidently, they were going to sell the notion of safety by not allowing them to move about without a mahout on their shoulders all the time. What do we do now?"

"That's what I've been thinking," muttered Donovan. "We can't go out on the surface, with a robot or without. Oh, for the love of Pete"—and he snapped his fingers twice. He grew excited. "Give me that map you've got. I haven't studied it for two hours for nothing. This is a mining station. What's wrong with using the tunnels?"

The mining station was a black circle on the map, and the light dotted lines that were tunnels stretched out about it in spider-web fashion.

Donovan studied the list of symbols at the bottom of the map. "Look," he said, "the small black dots are openings to the surface, and here's one maybe three miles away from the selenium pool. There's a number here—you'd think they'd write larger—13a. If the robots know their way around here—"

Powell shot the question and received the dull "Yes, Master," in reply. "Get your insosuit," Powell said with satisfaction.

It was the first time either had worn the insosuits —which marked one time more than either had expected to upon their arrival the day before—and they tested their limb movements uncomfortably.

The insosuits were far bulkier and far uglier than the regulation space suits, but withal considerably lighter, due to the fact that they were entirely non-metallic in composition. Composed of heat-resistant plastic and chemically treated cork layers, and equipped with a desiccating unit to keep the air bone-dry, the insosuits could withstand the full glare of Mercury's sun for twenty minutes. Five to ten minutes more, as well, without actually killing the occupant.

And still the robot's hands formed the stirrup, nor did he betray the slightest atom of surprise at the grotesque figure into which Powell had been converted.

Powell's radio-harshened voice boomed out: "Are you ready to take us to Exit 13a?"

"Yes, Master."

Good, thought Powell; they might lack radio control but at least they were fitted for radio reception. "Mount one or the other, Mike," he said to Donovan.

He placed a foot in the improvised stirrup and swung upward. He found the seat comfortable; there was the humped back of the robot, evidently shaped for the purpose, a shallow groove along each shoulder for the thighs and two elongated "ears" whose purpose now seemed obvious.

Powell seized the ears and twisted the head. His mount turned ponderously. "Lead on Macduff." But he did not feel at all lighthearted.

The gigantic robots moved slowly, with mechanical precision, through the doorway that cleared their heads by a scant foot, so that the two men had to duck hurriedly, along a narrow corridor in which their unhurried footsteps boomed monotonously and into the air lock.

The long, airless tunnel that stretched to a pinpoint before them brought home forcefully to Powell the exact magnitude of the task accomplished by the first expedition, with their crude robots and their start-from-scratch necessities. They might have been a failure, but their failure was a good deal better than the usual run of the System's successes.

The robots plodded onward with a pace that never varied and with footsteps that never lengthened.

Powell said, "Notice that these tunnels are blazing with lights and that the temperature is Earth-normal. It's probably been like this all the ten years that this place has remained empty."

"How's that?"

"Cheap energy; cheapest in the System. Sun power, you know, and on Mercury's Sunside, sun power is *something*. That's why the station was built in the sunlight rather than in the shadow of a mountain. It's really a huge energy converter. The heat is turned into electricity, light, mechanical work and what have you; so that energy is supplied and the Station is cooled in a simultaneous process."

"Look," said Donovan. "This is all very educational, but would you mind changing the subject? It so happens that this conversion of energy that you talk about is carried on by the photocell banks mainly—and that is a tender subject with me at the moment."

Powell grunted vaguely, and when Donovan broke the resulting silence, it was to change the subject completely. "Listen, Greg. What the devil's wrong with Speedy, anyway? I can't understand it."

It's not easy to shrug shoulders in an insosuit, but Powell tried it. "I don't know, Mike. You know he's perfectly adapted to a Mercurian environment. Heat doesn't mean anything to him and he's built for the light gravity and the broken ground. He's foolproof —or, at least, he should be."

Silence fell. This time, silence that lasted.

"Master," said the robot, "we are here."

"Eh?" Powell snapped out of a semidrowse. "Well, get us out of here—out to the surface."

They found themselves in a tiny substation, empty, airless, ruined. Donovan had inspected a jagged hole in the upper reaches of one of the walls by the light of his pocket flash.

"Meteorite, do you suppose?" he had asked.

Powell shrugged. "To hell with that. It doesn't matter. Let's get out."

A towering cliff of a black, basaltic rock cut off the sunlight, and the deep night shadow of an airless world surrounded them. Before them, the shadow reached out and ended in knife-edge abruptness into an all-but-unbearable blaze of white light that glittered from myriad crystals along a rocky ground.

"Space!" gasped Donovan. "It looks like snow." And it did.

Powell's eyes swept the jagged glitter of Mercury to the horizon and winced at the gorgeous brilliance.

"This must be an unusual area," he said. "The general albedo of Mercury is low and most of the soil is gray pumice. Something like the Moon, you know. Beautiful, isn't it?"

He was thankful for the light filters in their visiplates. Beautiful or not, a look at the sunlight through straight glass would have blinded them inside of half a minute.

Donovan was looking at the spring thermometer on his wrist. "Holy smokes, the temperature is eighty centigrade!"

Powell checked his own and said: "Um-m-m. A little high. Atmosphere, you know."

"On Mercury? Are you nuts?"

"Mercury isn't really airless," explained Powell, in absent-minded fashion. He was adjusting the binocular attachments to his visiplate, and the bloated fingers of the insosuit were clumsy at it. "There is a thin exhalation that clings to its surface—vapors of the more volatile elements and compounds that are heavy enough for Mercurian gravity to retain. You know: selenium, iodine, mercury, gallium, potassium, bismuth, volatile oxides. The vapors sweep into the shadows and condense, giving up heat. It's a sort of gigantic still. In fact, if you use your flash, you'll probably find that the side of the cliff is covered with, say, hoar-sulfur, or maybe quicksilver dew.

"It doesn't matter, though. Our suits can stand a measly eighty indefinitely."

Powell had adjusted the binocular attachments, so that he seemed as eye-stalked as a snail.

Donovan watched tensely. "See anything?"

The other did not answer immediately, and when he did, his voice was anxious and thoughtful. "There's a dark spot on the horizon that might be the selenium pool. It's in the right place. But I don't see Speedy."

Powell clambered upward in an instinctive striving for better view, till he was standing in unsteady fashion upon his robot's shoulders. Legs straddled wide, eyes straining, he said: "I think . . . I think— yes, it's definitely he. He's coming this way."

Donovan followed the pointing finger. He had no binoculars, but there was a tiny moving dot, black against the blazing brilliance of the crystalline ground.

"I see him," he yelled. "Let's get going!"

Powell had hopped down into a sitting position on the robot again, and his suited hand slapped against the Gargantuan's barrel chest. "Get going!"

"Giddy-ap," yelled Donovan, and thumped his heels, spur fashion.

The robots started off, the regular thudding of their footsteps silent in the airlessness, for the non-metallic fabric of the insosuits did not transmit sound. There was only a rhythmic vibration just below the border of actual hearing.

"Faster," yelled Donovan. The rhythm did not change.

"No use," cried Powell, in reply. "These junk heaps are only geared to one speed. Do you think they're equipped with selective flexors?"

They had burst through the shadow, and the sunlight came down in a white-hot wash and poured liquidly about them.

Donovan ducked involuntarily. "Wow! Is it imagination or do I feel heat?"

"You'll feel more presently," was the grim reply. "Keep your eye on Speedy."

Robot SPD 13 was near enough to be seen in detail now. His graceful, streamlined body threw out blazing highlights as he loped with easy speed across the broken ground. His name was derived from his serial initials, of course, but it was apt, nevertheless, for the SPD models were among the fastest robots turned out by the United States Robot & Mechanical Men Corp.

"Hey, Speedy," howled Donovan, and waved a frantic hand.

"Speedy!" shouted Powell. "Come here!"

The distance between the men and the errant

robot was being cut down momentarily—more by the efforts of Speedy than the slow plodding of the fifty-year-old antique mounts of Donovan and Powell.

They were close enough now to notice that Speedy's gait included a peculiar rolling stagger, a noticeable side-to-side lurch—and then, as Powell waved his hand again and sent maximum juice into his compact head-set radio sender, in preparation for another shout, Speedy looked up and saw them.

Speedy hopped to a halt and remained standing for a moment—with just a tiny, unsteady weave, as though he were swaying in a light wind.

Powell yelled, "All right, Speedy. Come here, boy."

Whereupon Speedy's robot voice sounded in Powell's earphones for the first time.

It said, "Hot dog, let's play games. You catch me and I catch you; no love can cut our knife in two. For I'm Little Buttercup, sweet Little Buttercup. Whoops!" Turning on his heel, he sped off in the direction from which he had come, with a speed and fury that kicked up gouts of baked dust.

And his last words as he receded into the distance were, "There grew a little flower 'neath a great oak tree," followed by a curious metallic clicking that *might* have been a robotic equivalent of a hiccup.

Donovan said weakly: "Where did he pick up the Gilbert and Sullivan? Say, Greg, he . . . he's drunk or something."

"If you hadn't told me," was the bitter response, "I'd never realize it. Let's get back to the cliff. I'm roasting."

It was Powell who broke the desperate silence. "In the first place," he said, "Speedy isn't drunk—not in the human sense—because he's a robot, and robots don't get drunk. However, there's *something* wrong with him which is the robotic equivalent of drunkenness."

"To me, he's drunk," stated Donovan, emphatically, "and all I know is that he thinks we're playing games. And we're not. It's a matter of life and very gruesome death."

"All right. Don't hurry me. A robot's only a robot. Once we find out what's wrong with him, we can fix it and go on."

"*Once*," said Donovan, sourly.

Powell ignored him. "Speedy is perfectly adapted to normal Mercurian environment. But this region"—and his arm swept wide—"is definitely abnormal. There's our clue. Now where do these crystals come from? They might have formed from a slowly cooling liquid; but where would you get liquid so hot that it would cool in Mercury's sun?"

"Volcanic action," suggested Donovan, instantly, and Powell's body tensed.

"Out of the mouths of sucklings," he said in a small, strange voice and remained very still for five minutes.

Then, he said, "Listen, Mike, what did you say to Speedy when you sent him after the selenium?"

Donovan was taken aback. "Well damn it—I don't know. I just told him to get it."

"Yes, I know. But how? Try to remember the exact words."

"I said . . . uh . . . I said: 'Speedy, we need some

selenium. You can get it such-and-such a place. Go get it.' That's all. What more did you want me to say?"

"You didn't put any urgency into the order, did you?"

"What for? It was pure routine."

Powell sighed. "Well, it can't be helped now—but we're in a fine fix." He had dismounted from his robot, and was sitting, back against the cliff. Donovan joined him and they linked arms. In the distance the burning sunlight seemed to wait cat-and-mouse for them, and just next to them, the two giant robots were invisible but for the dull red of their photoelectric eyes that stared down at them, unblinking, unwavering, and unconcerned.

Unconcerned! As was all this poisonous Mercury, as large in jinx as it was small in size.

Powell's radio voice was tense in Donovan's ear: "Now, look, let's start with the three fundamental Rules of Robotics—the three rules that are built most deeply into a robot's positronic brain." In the darkness, his gloved fingers ticked off each point.

"We have: One, a robot may not injure a human being, or, through inaction, allow a human being to come to harm."

"Right!"

"Two," continued Powell, "a robot must obey the orders given it by human beings except where such orders would conflict with the First Law."

"Right!"

"And three, a robot must protect its own existence as long as such protection does not conflict with the First or Second Laws."

"Right! Now where are we?"

"Exactly at the explanation. The conflict between the various rules is ironed out by the different positronic potentials in the brain. We'll say that a robot is walking into danger and knows it. The automatic potential that Rule 3 sets up turns him back. But suppose you *order* him to walk into that danger. In that case, Rule 2 sets up a counterpotential higher than the previous one and the robot follows orders at the risk of existence."

"Well, I know that. What about it?"

"Let's take Speedy's case. Speedy is one of the latest models, extremely specialized, and as expensive as a battleship. It's not a thing to be lightly destroyed."

"So?"

"So Rule 3 has been strengthened—that was specifically mentioned, by the way, in the advance notices on the SPD models—so that his allergy to danger is unusually high. At the same time, when you sent him out after the selenium, you gave him his order casually and without special emphasis, so that the Rule 2 potential set-up was rather weak. Now, hold on; I'm just stating facts."

"All right, go ahead. I think I get it."

"You see how it works, don't you? There's some sort of danger centering at the selenium pool. It increases as he approaches, and at a certain distance from it the Rule 3 potential, unusually high to start with, exactly balances the Rule 2 potential, unusually low to start with."

Donovan rose to his feet in excitement. "And it

strikes an equilibrium. I see. Rule 3 drives him back and Rule 2 drives him forward—"

"So he follows a circle around the selenium pool, staying on the locus of all points of potential equilibrium. And unless we do something about it, he'll stay on that circle forever, giving us the good old runaround." Then, more thoughtfully: "And that, by the way, is what makes him drunk. At potential equilibrium, half the positronic paths of his brain are out of kilter. I'm not a robot specialist, but that seems obvious. Probably he's lost control of just those parts of his voluntary mechanism that a human drunk has. Ve-e-ery pretty."

"But what's the danger? If we knew what he was running from—"

"*You* suggested it. Volcanic action. Somewhere right above the selenium pool is a seepage of gas from the bowels of Mercury. Sulphur dioxide, carbon dioxide—and carbon monoxide. Lots of it—and at this temperature."

Donovan gulped audibly. "Carbon monoxide plus iron gives the volatile iron carbonyl."

"And a robot," added Powell, "is essentially iron." Then, grimly: "There's nothing like deduction. We've determined everything about our problem but the solution. We can't get the selenium ourselves. It's still too far. We can't send these robot horses, because they can't go themselves, and they can't carry us fast enough to keep us from crisping. And we can't catch Speedy, because the dope thinks we're playing games, and he can run sixty miles to our four."

"If one of us goes," began Donovan, tentatively, "and comes back cooked, there'll still be the other."

"Yes," came the sarcastic reply, "it would be a most tender sacrifice—except that a person would be in no condition to give orders before he ever reaches the pool, and I don't think the robots would ever turn back to the cliff without orders. Figure it out! We're two or three miles from the pool—call it two—the robot travels at four miles an hour; and we can last twenty minutes in our suits. It isn't only the heat, remember. Solar radiation out here in the ultraviolet and below is *poison*."

"Um-m-m," said Donovan, "ten minutes short."

"As good as an eternity. And another thing. In order for Rule 3 potential to have stopped Speedy where it did, there must be an appreciable amount of carbon monoxide in the metal-vapor atmosphere —and there must be an appreciable corrosive action therefore. He's been out hours now—and how do we know when a knee joint, for instance, won't be thrown out of kilter and keel him over. It's not only a question of thinking—we've got to think *fast!*"

Deep, dark, dank, dismal silence!

Donovan broke it, voice trembling in an effort to keep itself emotionless. He said, "As long as we can't increase Rule 2 potential by giving further orders, how about working the other way? If we increase the danger, we increase Rule 3 potential and drive him backward."

Powell's visiplate had turned toward him in a silent question.

"You see," came the cautious explanation, "all

we need to do to drive him out of his rut is to increase the concentration of carbon monoxide in his vicinity. Well, back at the station there's a complete analytical laboratory."

"Naturally," assented Powell. "It's a mining station."

"All right. There must be pounds of oxalic acid for calcium precipitations."

"Holy space! Mike, you're a genius."

"So-so," admitted Donovan, modestly. "It's just a case of remembering that oxalic acid on heating decomposes into carbon dioxide, water, and good old carbon monoxide. College chem, you know."

Powell was on his feet and had attracted the attention of one of the monster robots by the simple expedient of pounding the machine's thigh.

"Hey," he shouted, "can you throw?"

"Master?"

"Never mind." Powell damned the robot's molasses-slow brain. He scrabbled up a jagged brick-size rock. "Take this," he said, "and hit the patch of bluish crystals just across that crooked fissure. You see it?"

Donovan pulled at his shoulder. "Too far, Greg. It's almost half a mile off."

"Quiet," replied Powell. "It's a case of Mercurian gravity and a steel throwing arm. Watch, will you?"

The robot's eyes were measuring the distance with machinely accurate stereoscopy. His arm adjusted itself to the weight of the missile and drew back. In the darkness, the robot's motions went unseen, but there was a sudden thumping sound as he shifted his weight, and seconds later the rock flew blackly into the sunlight. There was no air resistance to slow it down, nor wind to turn it aside— and when it hit the ground it threw up crystals precisely in the center of the "blue patch."

Powell yelled happily and shouted, "Let's go back after the oxalic acid, Mike."

And as they plunged into the ruined substation on the way back to the tunnels, Donovan said grimly, "Speedy's been hanging about on this side of the selenium pool, ever since we chased after him. Did you see him?"

"Yes."

"I guess he wants to play games. Well, we'll play his games!"

They were back hours later, with three-liter jars of the white chemical and a pair of long faces. The photocell banks were deteriorating more rapidly than had seemed likely. The two steered their robots into the sunlight and toward the waiting Speedy in silence and with grim purpose.

Speedy galloped slowly toward them. "Here we are again. *Whee!* I've made a little list, the piano organist; all people who eat peppermint and puff it in your face."

"We'll puff something in *your* face," muttered Donovan. "He's limping, Greg."

"I noticed that," came the low, worried response. "The monoxide'll get him yet, if we don't hurry."

They were approaching cautiously now, almost sidling, to refrain from setting off the thoroughly irrational robot. Powell was too far off to tell, of course, but even already he could have sworn the crack-brained Speedy was setting himself for a spring.

"Let her go," he gasped. "Count three! One—two—"

Two steel arms drew back and snapped forward simultaneously and two glass jars whirled forward in towering parallel arcs, gleaming like diamonds in the impossible sun. And in a pair of soundless puffs, they hit the ground behind Speedy in crashes that sent the oxalic acid flying like dust.

In the full heat of Mercury's sun, Powell knew it was fizzing like soda water.

Speedy turned to stare, then backed away from it slowly—and as slowly gathered speed. In fifteen seconds, he was leaping directly toward the two humans in an unsteady canter.

Powell did not get Speedy's words just then, though he heard something that resembled, "Lover's professions when uttered in Hessians."

He turned away. "Back to the cliff, Mike. He's out of the rut and he'll be taking orders now. I'm getting hot."

They jogged toward the shadow at the slow monotonous pace of their mounts, and it was not until they had entered it and felt the sudden coolness settle softly about them that Donovan looked back. *"Greg!"*

Powell looked and almost shrieked. Speedy was moving slowly now—so slowly—and in the *wrong direction*. He was drifting; drifting back into his rut; and he was picking up speed. He looked dreadfully close, and dreadfully unreachable, in the binoculars.

Donovan shouted wildly, "After him!" and thumped his robot into its pace, but Powell called him back.

"You won't catch him, Mike—it's no use." He fidgeted on his robot's shoulders and clenched his fist in tight impotence. "Why the devil do I see these things five seconds after it's all over? Mike, we've wasted hours."

"We need more oxalic acid," declared Donovan, stolidly. "The concentration wasn't high enough."

"Seven tons of it wouldn't have been enough—and we haven't the hours to spare to get it, even if it were, with the monoxide chewing him away. Don't you see what it is, Mike?"

And Donovan said flatly, "No."

"We were only establishing new equilibriums. When we created new monoxide and increased Rule 3 potential, he moved backward till he was in balance again—and when the monoxide drifted away, he moved forward, and again there was balance."

Powell's voice sounded thoroughly wretched. "It's the same old runaround. We can push at Rule 2 and pull at Rule 3 and we can't get anywhere—we can only change the position of balance. We've got to get outside both rules." And then he pushed his robot closer to Donovan's so that they were sitting face to face, dim shadows in the darkness, and he whispered, "Mike!"

"Is it the finish?"—dully. "I suppose we go back

to the station, wait for the banks to fold, shake hands, take cyanide, and go out like gentlemen." He laughed shortly.

"Mike," repeated Powell earnestly, "we've got to get Speedy."

"I know."

"Mike," once more, and Powell hesitated before continuing. "There's always Rule 1. I thought of it —earlier—but it's desperate."

Donovan looked up and his voice livened. *"We're* desperate."

"All right. According to Rule 1, a robot can't see a human come to harm because of his own inaction. Two and 3 can't stand against it. They *can't*, Mike."

"Even when the robot is half cra— Well, he's drunk. You know he is."

"It's the chances you take."

"Cut it. What are you going to do?"

"I'm going out there now and see what Rule 1 will do. If it won't break the balance, then what the devil—it's either now or three-four days from now."

"Hold on, Greg. There are human rules of behavior, too. You don't go out there just like that. Figure out a lottery, and give me *my* chance."

"All right. First to get the cube of fourteen goes." And almost immediately, "Twenty-seven forty-four!"

Donovan felt his robot stagger at a sudden push by Powell's mount and then Powell was off into the sunlight. Donovan opened his mouth to shout, and then clicked it shut. Of course, the damn fool had worked out the cube of fourteen in advance, and on purpose. Just like him.

The sun was hotter than ever and Powell felt a maddening itch in the small of his back. Imagination, probably, or perhaps hard radiation beginning to tell even through the insosuit.

Speedy was watching him, without a word of Gilbert and Sullivan gibberish as greeting. Thank God for that! But he daren't get too close.

He was three hundred yards away when Speedy began backing, a step at a time, cautiously—and Powell stopped. He jumped from his robot's shoulders and landed on the crystalline ground with a light thump and a flying of jagged fragments.

He proceeded on foot, the ground gritty and slippery to his steps, the low gravity causing him difficulty. The soles of his feet tickled with warmth. He cast one glance over his shoulder at the blackness of the cliff's shadow and realized that he had come too far to return—either by himself or by the help of his antique robot. It was Speedy or nothing now, and the knowledge of that constricted his chest.

Far enough! He stopped.

"Speedy," he called. "Speedy!"

The sleek, modern robot ahead of him hesitated and halted his backward steps, then resumed them.

Powell tried to put a note of pleading into his voice, and found it didn't take much acting. "Speedy, I've got to get back to the shadow or the sun'll get me. It's life or death, Speedy. I need you."

Speedy took one step forward and stopped. He spoke, but at the sound Powell groaned, for it was, "When you're lying awake with a dismal headache and repose is tabooed—" It trailed off there, and

Powell took time out for some reason to murmur, "Iolanthe."

It was roasting hot! He caught a movement out of the corner of his eye, and whirled dizzily; then stared in utter astonishment, for the monstrous robot on which he had ridden was moving—moving toward him, and without a rider.

He was talking: "Pardon, Master. I must not move without a Master upon me, but you are in danger."

Or course, Rule 1 potential above everything. But he didn't want that clumsy antique; he wanted Speedy. He walked away and motioned frantically: "I order you to stay away. I *order* you to stop!"

It was quite useless. You could not beat Rule 1 potential. The robot said stupidly, "You are in danger, Master."

Powell looked about him desperately. He couldn't see clearly. His brain was in a heated whirl; his breath scorched when he breathed, and the ground all about him was a shimmering haze.

He called a last time, desperately: "*Speedy!* I'm dying, damn you! Where are you? Speedy, I *need* you."

He was still stumbling backward in a blind effort to get away from the giant robot he didn't want, when he felt steel fingers on his arms, and a worried, apologetic voice of metallic timbre in his ears.

"Holy smokes, boss, what are you doing here? And what am *I* doing—I'm so confused—"

"Never mind," murmured Powell, weakly. "Get me to the shadow of the cliff—and hurry!" There was one last feeling of being lifted into the air and a sensation of rapid motion and burning heat, and he passed out.

He woke with Donovan bending over him and smiling anxiously. "How are you, Greg?"

"Fine!" came the response. "Where's Speedy?"

"Right here. I sent him out to one of the other selenium pools—with orders to get that selenium at all cost this time. He got it back in forty-two minutes and three seconds. I timed him. He still hasn't finished apologizing for the runaround he gave us. He's scared to come near you for fear of what you'll say."

"Drag him over," ordered Powell. "It wasn't his fault." He held out a hand and gripped Speedy's metal paw. "It's OK, Speedy." Then, to Donovan, "You know, Mike, I was just thinking—"

"Yes!"

"Well,"—he rubbed his face—the air was so delightfully cool, "you know that when we get things set up here and Speedy put through his field tests, they're going to send us to the Space Stations next—"

"No!"

"Yes! At least that's what old lady Calvin told me just before we left, and I didn't say anything about it, because I was going to fight the whole idea."

"Fight it?" cried Donovan. "But—"

"I know. It's all right with me now. Two hundred seventy-three degrees Centigrade below zero. Won't it be a pleasure?"

"Space Station," said Donovan, "here I come."

Earth for Inspiration

Clifford D. Simak

Clifford D. Simak is today regarded as one of the best half-dozen active science fiction writers. He has won the two highest awards possible in the science fiction world: The International Fantasy Award in 1952 for the best novel of the year, City, *and the "Hugo" (a cast-iron spaceship which is the science fiction world's "Oscar") in 1959 for the best novelette of the year,* The Big Front Yard. *A lifelong newspaperman, Simak became news editor of the* Minneapolis Star *in 1949, and he was recently assigned the task of developing a science news program for that paper in an age when scientific advancement frequently makes headlines. Simak's stories reflect a wholesomeness and optimism which is all too rare in this tense modern age. His descriptive backgrounds and avoidance of clichés indicate Simak's vast knowledge of science fiction lore.*

Earth for Inspiration

PHILBERT WAS LOST. Likewise, he was frightened. That, in itself, was frightening, for Philbert was a robot and robots should have no emotions.

Philbert revolved that inside his brain case for many minutes, trying to figure it out. But there was no logic in it.

All around stretched the death and desolation that was Old Earth. High overhead the brick-red Sun shone dully in an ink-black sky, for the atmosphere was nearly gone, and the stars shone with a hard, bright glitter. The scraggly vegetation, fighting hard for life in a world where but little life was left, seemed to cower beneath a sense of ingrained futility.

Philbert stretched out his right leg and it squeaked. The knee joint had gone bad many hours before. Some sand had gotten into it, probably when he had fallen and broken his orientation plate. That was why he was lost. The three eyes in the top of Philbert's head studied the stars intently.

"I wish," said Philbert, his voice box rasping from lack of lubrication, "that I knew something about the constellations. The boss claimed men used to navigate by them. Well, that's wishful thinking." He had to find oil or he was sunk. If only he could retrace his steps to the shattered spaceship and the equally shattered body of the man within it, he would find plenty there. But he couldn't retrace his steps, for he had no idea where the wreckage lay.

All he could do was keep plodding on, hoping to find the lone space port. Once each month the regular space run brought pilgrims and tourists to the old shrines and legendary places of mankind's first home. Or he might stumble on one of the primitive tribes that still lived on Old Earth.

He went on, the bad knee squeaking. The Sun slid slowly down the west. The Moon rose, a monstrous, pock-marked world. Philbert's shadow lurched ahead of him as he crossed eroded, worn-down mountains, trudged dune-filled deserts and salt-caked sea beds. But there was no sign of living things.

The knee squeaked louder. Finally he took it apart, unfastened the other joint and scraped some grease from it for the squeaking knee. In a few days both knees were squeaking. He took apart his arms, one at a time, and robbed them of their grease. It didn't matter if the arms ceased functioning, but those legs just had to move!

Next it was a hip joint that complained, then

both hips, and finally the ankle joints. Philbert pushed forward, metal howling with dryness, walking less steadily each day.

He found a camping site, but the men were gone. The water had given out, so the tribe had moved.

The right leg was dragging now and fear hammered at him. "I'm getting batty," he moaned. "I'm beginning to imagine things, and only humans do that. Only humans—"

His voice box croaked and rasped and slipped a cog. The leg gave out and he crawled. Then his arms gave out and he lay still. The sand hissed against his metal body.

"Someone will find me," Philbert rattled hoarsely.

But no one found him. Philbert's body became a rusted hulk. His hearing went first and after that his eyes failed one by one. His body became flakes of dull red metal. But inside its almost indestructible case, lubricated by sealed-in oil, Philbert's brain still clicked.

He still lived, or rather he existed. He could neither see nor hear nor move nor speak. He was nothing more than a complex thought suspended in an abyss of nothingness. Man's life expectancy was 10,000 years, but a robot's was dependent only on accident.

The years stretched into centuries and the centuries rolled into eons. Philbert thought dutifully, solved great problems, puzzled out correct actions under an endless set of circumstances. But futility at last caught up with him.

Bored to desperation, rebelling at dusty logic, he

reasoned out a logical solution that effectively ended, not without some misgivings, the need for logic. While he had been an associate of mankind, it had been his duty to be logical. Now he was no longer associated with Man. Therefore, serving no purpose, there was no need of his logic.

Philbert was, by nature, thorough. He never did a thing by halves. He built up impossible situations, devised great travels and adventures, accepted shaky premises and theories, dallied with metaphysical speculation. He wandered to improbable dimensions, conversed with strange beings that lived on unknown worlds, battled with vicious entities that spawned outside the pale of time and space, rescued civilizations tottering on the brink of horrible destruction.

The years galloped on and on, but Philbert didn't notice. He was having him a time.

Jerome Duncan regarded the rejection slip sourly, picked it up gingerly, and deciphered the editorial scrawl.

Not convincing. Too little science. Situations too commonplace. Characters have no life. Sorry.

"You sure outdid yourself this time!" snarled Duncan, addressing the scrawl.

Jenkins, the soft-footed robot valet, slid into the room.

"Another one, sir?" he asked.

Duncan jumped at the sound of the voice, then snapped at the robot:

"Jenkins, quit sneaking up on me. You make me nervous."

"I beg your pardon, sir," said Jenkins stiffly. "I wasn't sneaking up on you. I was just observing that another manuscript came back."

"What if it did? Lots of them have been coming back."

"That's just the point, sir. They never used to come back. You wrote some of the finest science fiction the Galaxy has ever known. Real classics, sir, if I do say so myself. Your *Robots Triumphant* won the annual award, sir, and—"

Duncan brightened. "Yeah, that was some yarn, wasn't it? All the robots wrote in and swamped that old sourpuss of an editor with letters praising it. But the robots would be the ones to eat it up. It was a story about them, giving them a break."

He glanced sadly at the rejection slip and shook his head.

"But no more, Jenkins. Duncan is on the skids. And yet readers keep asking about me. 'When is Duncan going to write another like *Robots Triumphant?*' But the editor keeps sending my stuff back. 'Not convincing,' he says. 'Not enough science. Characters no good!' "

"May I make a suggestion, sir?"

"Okay," sighed Duncan. "Go ahead and make one."

"It's this way, sir," said Jenkins. "If you will pardon me, your stories don't sound convincing any more."

"Yeah? What am I going to do about it?"

"Why don't you visit some of these places you are writing about?" the robot suggested. "Why don't you take a vacation and see if you can't gather some local color and some inspiration?" Duncan scratched his head.

"Maybe you got something there, Jenkins," he admitted. He glanced at the returned manuscript, thumbed through its pages.

"This one should have sold. It's an Old Earth story and they're always popular."

He shoved the manuscript away from him and stood up.

"Jenkins, call up Galactic Transportation and find out the schedule to Old Earth."

"But the Old Earth run was discontinued a thousand years ago," protested Jenkins.

"There are shrines there that Man has been going to see for millions of years."

"It seems, sir," said Jenkins, "that no one's interested in shrines any more."

"All right, then," stated Duncan. "Scram out of here and charter a ship and get together some camping equipment."

"Camping equipment, sir?"

"Camping equipment. We're going to go back to Old Earth and pitch a tent there. We're going to soak up atmosphere until it runs out of our ears."

He glared viciously at the scrawl on the rejection slip.

"I'll show that old—"

The news bell tinkled softly and a blue light glowed in the wall panel. When Duncan pressed a stud, a newspaper shot out of a tube onto his desk. Swiftly he flipped it open and read the glaring scarlet headlines:

ROBOT RUSTLERS STRIKE AGAIN

Duncan tossed the paper to one side in disgust.

"They're going nuts about those rustlers," he said. "Who would kidnap a few robots. Maybe the robots are running away."

"But they wouldn't run away," insisted Jenkins. "Not those robots, sir. I knew some of them. They were loyal to their masters."

"It's just newspaper build-up," declared Duncan. "They're trying to get more circulation."

"But it's happening all over the Galaxy, sir," Jenkins reminded him. "The papers say it looks like the work of an organized gang. Stealing robots and selling them again could be a profitable business, sir."

"If it is," grunted Duncan, "the CBI will get them. Nobody's ever ducked that bunch of sleuths for long."

Old Hank Wallace stared skyward, muttering in his beard.

"By thunder," he suddenly yelped, "a ship at last!"

He hobbled toward the port control shack, heaved down the levers that lighted up the field, then stepped out to have another look. The ship came slanting down, touched the concrete lightly and skidded to a stop.

Hank shuffled forward, the breath whistling in his oxygen mask. A man, equipped with mask and swathed in heavy furs, stepped from the ship. He was followed by a robot, loaded down with packs and bundles.

"Howdy, there," yelled Hank. "Welcome to Old Earth."

The man regarded him curiously.

"We didn't think we'd find anyone here," he said.

Hank bristled. "Why not? This is a Galactic Transport station. You always find someone here. Service at all hours."

"But this station has been abandoned," explained Jerome Duncan. "The run was canceled a thousand years ago."

The old man let the information sink in.

"You're sure of that?" he asked. "You're sure they canceled the run?"

Duncan nodded.

"Dagnabit!" exploded Hank. "I knew there was something wrong. I thought there might have been a war."

"Jenkins," ordered Duncan, "get that camping stuff out of the ship as fast as you can."

"It's a dirty trick," lamented Hank. "A doggone dirty trick. Letting a man hang around here for a thousand years waiting for a ship."

Hank and Duncan sat side by side, chairs tilted back against the station wall, watching the Sun slip into the west.

"If it's atmosphere and color you're looking for," said Hank, "you sure ought to find it here. Once this was a green land, where a great civilization got its start. You kind of feel something almost sacred in this place when you get to know it. Mother Earth, they used to call it, way back in those early days before they left it behind and went out into the Galaxy. For centuries, though, they came back to visit the shrines."

He shook his head sadly.

"But they've forgotten all that now. History doesn't give Old Earth more than a paragraph or two. Just says it was the place where mankind arose. I heard once that there was a fellow who even claimed Man didn't come from Earth at all, but from some other planet."

"These last thousand years must have been lonesome ones," suggested Duncan.

"Not so bad," the old man told him. "At first I had Wilbur. He was my robot, and he was a lot of company. We used to sit around and chew the fat. But Wilbur went off his clock, cog slipped or something. Started acting queer and I got scared of him. So I watched for my chance and disconnected him. Then, just to make sure, I took the brain case out of his body. It's in there on the shelf. I take it down and polish it every now and then. Wilbur was a good robot."

From outside the station came a thump and clatter.

"Hey!" yelled Duncan. "What's going on in there?"

"I just found a robot's body, sir," called Jenkins. "I must have knocked it over."

"You know you knocked it over," snapped Duncan. "That's Wilbur's body. Put it back where it belongs."

"Yes, sir," said Jenkins.

"If you're looking for characters," continued Hank, "you ought to visit an old ocean depth about five hundred miles from here. A tribe is living there, one of the last left on Old Earth. They're the ones that just weren't worth the space they'd take up in ships when mankind left the Earth. But that was millions of years ago. There aren't many of them left now. The only place where water and air are left is in the old sea depths. The strongest tribes grabbed those long ago and drove out the weaker tribes."

"What happened to the weaker tribes?" asked Duncan.

"They died," said Hank. "You can't live without water and air, you know. They don't live long, anyway. Hundred years is about their limit, maybe less. There have been twelve chiefs in the last thousand years that I know of. An old duffer that calls himself the 'Thunderer' rules the roost right now. Nothing but a bag of bones, and thunder hasn't been heard on Earth for five million years at least. But they're great on names like that. Great storytellers, too. They got some real hair-raisers."

The Thunderer let out a squeak of rage and got weakly to his feet. A band of urchins had rolled the ball that had hit his foot. They took to their heels, disappeared around the corner in a cloud of dust. Stiffly the Thunderer sat down again, groaning. He wiggled his toes, watching them intently, apparently surprised when they worked.

"Them dang kids will be the death of me," he grumbled. "No manners. When I was a youngster, my pappy would have whaled the living daylights out of me for a trick like that."

Jerome Duncan picked up the sphere.

"Where did they get this ball, Chief?" he asked.

"Out in the desert somewhere, I guess," said the Thunderer. "We used to find a lot of junk scattered around, especially on the old city sites. My tribe used to do a big business in it. Sold antiques to them fool tourists."

"But, Chief," protested Duncan, "this isn't just a piece of junk. This is a robot's brain case."

"Yeah?" piped the Thunderer.

"Sure," declared Duncan. "Look at the serial number, right down here." He bent his head closer to the number and whistled in surprise. "Look, Chief. This case is about three million years old! Only ten digits. This year's models have sixteen."

Duncan hefted the brain case in his cupped hands, considering.

"Might have an interesting story to tell," he said. "Might have been out there on the desert for a long time. Those old models all went to the junk pile centuries ago. Outdated, too many improvements. Emotions, for one thing. Three million years ago robots didn't have emotions. If we could connect it up—"

"You got a robot," the chief pointed out.

Duncan turned to Jenkins with a speculative look in his eyes, but Jenkins started backing away.

"No," he bleated. "Not that, sir! You can't do that to me."

"It would be just for a little while," Duncan coaxed.

"I don't like it," Jenkins said flatly. "I don't like it at all."

"Jenkins!" yelled Duncan. "You come here!"

Light lanced into Philbert's brain, a piercing, torturing light that shattered eons of shrouding nothingness. Alien visions swam across his senses. He tried to shut his eyes, but the mechanism of his brain was sluggish in response. The relentless light seared his eyes. Sound came to him, frightening sound. But he knew it should mean something to him.

Eye shutters down at last, he waited for his eyes to grow used to the light. He lifted the shutters just a bit. The light lashed at him again, but it was less vicious this time. Gradually he lifted the shutters, found his vision blurred and foggy. Sound was blasting at him again. Now it divided itself into words.

"Get up!"

The command drilled into his consciousness. Slowly, motor centers uncertainly taking up old tasks, he heaved himself erect. He staggered on his feet, fighting to keep his balance. It was terrifying, this sudden yanking of his consciousness from a dream world into a world of actuality. His eyes focused. Before him was a village of huts. Beyond that lay a tiny pond and ranges of barren hills that marched like stairs into the black sky where hung the large, red Sun. There were people in front of him, too. One man was different from the rest. He was dressed in furs, with an oxygen mask dangling on his chest.

"Who are you?" the man in furs asked.

"I am—" said Philbert, and then he stopped.

Who was he? He tried to remember, but his memory was engulfed by that world of fantasy and imagination in which he had so long existed. One word popped up, one tiny clue, and that was all.

"I am Philbert," he finally said.

"Do you know where you are?" asked the man. "How you came to be here? How long since you were alive?"

"I don't know," said Philbert.

"You see," squeaked the Thunderer, "he remembers nothing. He is a dunderhead."

"No, not that," Duncan disagreed. "He's been here too long. The years have wiped his memory clean."

The evening meal was over. The tribe squatted in a ring around the fire and listened to the Thunderer recite one of the tribal legends. It was a long tale with, Duncan suspected, but slight regard for truth. The Thunderer fixed him with a baleful eye, as if daring him to disbelieve.

"And so Angus took that critter from the stars in his bare hands and put its tail into its mouth and pushed. And it kept fighting all the time and trying to get loose. But Angus hung on and pushed that tail until the danged thing swallowed itself!"

The tribe murmured appreciatively. It was a good story. The murmur was broken by a raucous voice.

"Ah, shucks," jeered Philbert, "that ain't nothing!"

The tribe gasped in shocked amazement, growled with sudden anger. The Thunderer jumped as if he had been shot. Duncan started forward, a sharp command on his lips. The Thunderer stopped him with a raised hand.

"I suppose, you little whippersnapper," the chief piped at Philbert, "that you can tell a better one."

"You bet I can," Philbert stated. "And what's more, this one is the truth. These events really happened to me."

The Thunderer glared at him.

"All right," he growled, "go ahead and tell it. And it better be good. It better be plenty good."

Philbert started to talk. The tribesmen were hostile at first, but as he went along they snapped to abrupt attention. For Philbert was spinning a yarn that really was a yarn.

A screwball world had set out to conquer the rest of the Galaxy and used its very wackiness to accomplish its ends. Mankind, led by Philbert, of course, turned the tables on the conquerors and invented a synthetic screwball who upset all their plans.

Duncan sat enthralled, hanging on the words. Here was science fiction! The man who could write a tale like that would be hailed over the entire Galaxy as the master of his craft. His mind whirled, and the circle of faces blurred. Realization struck at him, left him pale.

The man who wrote that story would be himself!

Philbert had ended the tale, was stepping back

into the circle once again. Duncan grabbed the robot's arm.

"Philbert!" he shouted. "Where did you hear that story?"

"I didn't hear it," said Philbert. "It happened to me."

"But it couldn't have happened to you," protested Duncan. "If such a thing had happened, history would have mentioned it."

"It happened," Philbert insisted. "I am telling you the truth."

Duncan stared at the robot.

"Listen, Philbert," he urged, "did a lot of other things happen to you, too?"

"Sure," Philbert agreed cheerfully. "A lot of things. I went lots of places and did lots of things. Want me to tell about them?"

"Not right now," said Duncan hastily. "You come along with me."

Almost by main force, he shoved Philbert out of the circle and headed for the ship. Behind him a voice squeaked in rage.

"Hey, come back here!"

Duncan turned around. The Thunderer was on his feet, shaking clenched fists.

"You bring that robot back!" yelped the chief. "Don't you go sneaking off with him!"

"But he's my robot," said Duncan.

"You bring him back!" shrieked the old man. "He belongs to us. I guess we were the ones that found him. Think we're going to let you carry off the first good storyteller this tribe has had in five hundred years?"

"But, look here, Chief . . ."

"Dang you, bring him back! I'll sic the boys on you."

All the boys looked as if they would enjoy a little scrap. Duncan turned around to speak to Philbert, but Philbert was moving away rapidly.

"Hey, there!" yelled Duncan, but Philbert only went faster.

"Hey!" yelled the tribe in unison.

At the shout Philbert fairly split the wind. He streaked through the camp, across the flat, and skittered out of sight, disappearing in the darkness of the hills.

"Now see what you done!" shouted Duncan angrily. "You scared him off with all that yelling."

The Thunderer hobbled forward to shake a massive, hairy fist beneath Duncan's nose.

"Dang you!" he piped. "I ought to bust you wide open. Try to sneak off with that storyteller. You better get going before the boys decide to take you apart."

"But he was mine as much as yours," argued Duncan. "Maybe you found him, but it was my robot's body he was in and—"

"Stranger," cautioned the Thunderer fiercely, "you better get aboard that tin can of yours and clear out."

"Now look here," protested Duncan, "you can't run me off like this."

"Who says we can't?" gritted the old man.

Duncan saw the expectant, almost hopeful look on the faces of the watching tribesmen.

"Okay," he said. "I didn't really want to hang around, anyhow. You needn't get so tough."

Philbert's trail led straight across the desert. Old Hank grumbled in his beard.

"You're stark crazy, Duncan," he declared. "You can't catch this robot. Lord knows how far he went. He might not stop until he's halfway around the world."

"I have to catch him," Duncan said doggedly. "Don't you realize what he means to me? That robot is an encyclopedia of science fiction stories! That yarn he told this evening was better than anything I ever read. And he's got more of them. He told me so. He must have thought them up when he was lying out there in the sand. A couple of million years is a long time to lie around and think.

"If he were thinking of screwball scientific ideas all that time, he must be dripping with them. The beauty of it is that he thought about them so long, he forgot everything else he knew and thinks those wacky adventures of his are real. He really thinks he lived them."

"But, doggone it," panted Hank, "at least we could track him in the space ship. No use walking our legs down to the knees."

"You know what'll happen when we try to track him in the ship," said Duncan. "We'll go so fast that we won't even see the tracks. The ship isn't something you can throttle down. It has to go fast to escape gravity."

Jenkins stubbed his toe on a boulder and somersaulted in the sand with a thunderous clank and clatter. He pulled himself to his feet, making angry sounds.

"If he had to wear this body," Jenkins declared, "I can understand why Wilbur went nuts."

"You better be thankful that body was handy," snarled Duncan. "If it hadn't been, you'd still be disconnected. How would you like that?"

"No worse than stumbling around in this contraption, sir," said Jenkins.

"I was afraid at first," continued Duncan, "that maybe the old Thunderer would beat me to the draw and catch Philbert, but we don't have to worry about that any more. We're a good many miles from the tribal camp. They wouldn't wander this far."

"You wouldn't either, sir," said Jenkins crustily, "if you didn't have me to pack a couple of barrels of water for you. I don't like it. I'm a valet, not a pack horse."

Late in the afternoon, Jenkins was ahead. He stopped and yelled at them. They hurried forward to see what he had found.

The tracks of two other robots had joined Philbert's. There were signs of a scuffle and then the three tracks went angling up the dunes. Old Hank was horrified.

"But it can't be," he blurted, his whiskers waggling in exasperation. "There aren't any robots on Earth except Jenkins here and that crazy Philbert. There's Wilbur, of course, but he don't count no more."

"But there are," stated Duncan. "There are their three sets of tracks. It's plain as day what happened. The other two hid in wait for Philbert there behind those boulders and tackled him. He put up a little battle, but they finally got him tamed and led him off."

The three stood quietly staring at the tracks.

"How do you explain it?" whispered Hank.

"I'm not trying to explain it," snapped Duncan. "I'm going to follow them. I'm going to get Philbert if it's the last thing I ever do. I'm going to make that old sourpuss of an editor sit up when those yarns of mine start coming in. Philbert's got them. I just can't let him get away."

"I think you're full of moonshine," said Hank bitterly.

"So do I," agreed Jenkins. He added grudgingly: "Sir."

The trail led across a welter of dunes. Then it ducked into a rocky defile that slanted down into a fearsome valley, which went straight for a short distance and then abandoned itself to a series of tortuous turns.

"I don't like this place," whispered Hank hoarsely. "It downright smells of danger."

Duncan paid him no attention, went alertly forward. He slid around a sharp turn and stopped suddenly, his breath catching in his throat. The two behind came around the bend and bumped into him.

From the valley floor rose huge machines—mighty drills, mining equipment, shovels. All about were hundreds of robots!

"Let's get out of here!" quavered Hank.

They backed slowly away, silently, almost holding their breath. Jenkins, backing with them, stepped into a slight depression in the trail, lost his footing. Half a ton of hardware smacked against the rock with a bang that sent the echoes chasing between the narrow cliffs.

Robots suddenly began racing toward them, converging upon them in every direction.

"Boy," said Hank, "we're sure in for it now!"

Jenkins, on his feet again, cried out as they approached.

"I know some of those robots, sir! They are the ones the rustlers stole!"

"Who are the rustlers?" demanded Hank.

"We'll find out soon enough," said Duncan bitterly. "They're just about the toughest gang that ever roamed the Galaxy. Been stealing robots all over the place."

"And look at me," moaned Jenkins. "The boys will never let me forget it. Me, in a pile of junk like this."

"Keep your mouth shut," snapped Duncan, "and they'll never recognize you. If you go throwing yourself around any more, I'll disconnect that brain of yours and heave it out right in the middle of space."

"I didn't do it intentionally, sir," protested Jenkins. "This body is the most awkward thing I've ever seen. I just can't do a thing with it. Here they come!"

The robots were a milling mass in front of them.

One of the metal men stepped forward. He singled out Duncan and spoke to him.

"We're certainly glad to see you," he said. "We were hoping someone would find us."

"Find you?" asked Duncan. "Are you lost?"

The robot scuffed his feet and hung his head.

"Well, not exactly lost. We sort of pulled a boner."

"Look here," said Duncan impatiently. "What are you talking about? Aren't you the robots the rustlers stole?" "No, sir," the robot confessed. "You see, there aren't any rustlers."

"Aren't any rustlers!" exploded Duncan. "Well, if there aren't any rustlers, what are you fellows doing here?"

"We ran away, but it wasn't our fault. Not exactly, that is. You see, there was a science fiction writer—"

"What has a science fiction writer got to do with this?" roared Duncan.

"This science fiction writer wrote a story," explained the robot. "Fellow by the name of Jerome Duncan—"

Viciously Duncan kicked Jenkins in the shins and the robot gurgled, swallowing his words.

"He wrote a story called *Robots Triumphant*," the robot spokesman went on. "He told how a bunch of robots went out to build a civilization of their own. They were disgusted with the human race, thought Man had balled up just about everything. So they figgered they'd sneak off some place and start from scratch and build themselves a great civilization without any of mankind's faults."

The robot glanced sharply at Duncan.

"You don't think I'm stringing you, do you?" he asked.

"No," said Duncan. "I read that story myself. I thought it was pretty good."

"It was good," admitted the robot. "Too darned good. We believed it. It got us all hopped up, made us want to go out and do the things he told about." He stopped and fixed Duncan with a stare. "But if we had that Duncan guy now! Just let us catch him!"

Duncan's heart flopped down into his boots, but he kept his voice steady.

"Why, what's the matter, boys? Didn't the idea work out?"

"Work out!" the robot grated. "I'll tell the Galaxy it didn't. We sneaked off, a few at a time, and gathered at a place we had agreed on. When there was a shipload of us, we came here. We landed, unloaded our equipment, and then blew up the spaceship. That's what the robots did in the story, so no one could get sick of it and try to get away. Sort of sink or swim proposition. Understand?"

"Yes, I remember," said Duncan. "The robots in the story, I believe, even came back to Old Earth. Figured they ought to start out on the same planet mankind started on. Inspirational, sort of."

"Yeah," said the robot. "That all sounded swell in the story, but it didn't work so well. That fool writer forgot just one thing. He forgot that before Man left the Earth he stripped it clean. He'd pumped out all the oil and mined all the ore and chopped down all the timber. He cleaned the planet out. He didn't leave a thing. We've sunk wells, trying to get oil. There ain't a drop. The same with minerals. There isn't a thing here to start a civilization with.

"And the worst of it is that another bunch of the fellows are getting ready to go out to another old abandoned planet. We have to stop them, because they won't be any better off than we are. We're mighty glad you found us."

"But we weren't looking for you," stated Duncan. "We were looking for a robot called Philbert."

"We got him here," said the spokesman. "A couple of the boys saw him wandering around and thought he was one of our fellows trying to sneak off. They jumped him, but you can have him. We don't want him. He's batty. He almost drove us nuts telling us about the things he's done."

"Okay," said Duncan. "Trot him out."

"But what about us?"

"Well, what about you?"

"You're going to take us back, ain't you? You ain't going to leave us here?"

"I ought to let you guys stew in your own juice," said Duncan.

"Okay, then," said the robot. "We don't give you Philbert. We can't stand him around, but we can take him apart and throw him away."

"Hey, wait a minute!" yelled Duncan. "You can't do that."

"Take us back and you can have him," said the robot.

"But I haven't the room. All I have is just one spaceship that isn't nearly big enough for all of you."

"We'll fix that. We'll disconnect ourselves, leave our bodies behind. All you have to take are the brain cases."

"But look here, I can't. The CBI would nab me. They think you fellows were stolen by a gang they've been calling the 'Robot Rustlers.' They'll think I'm the head robot rustler."

"If they do," said the robot, "we'll testify for you. We'll come clean and save you. And if you do get us through without getting caught, you can claim you rescued us. We won't contradict you. Honest, mister, we'll do anything to get out of here."

Duncan considered. He didn't like the proposition, but there wasn't much that he could do.

"Well," asked the robot, "do we take Philbert apart or do you agree to take us?"

"All right," said Duncan, beaten. "Bring Philbert here."

Duncan waved the new issue of the magazine triumphantly at Philbert.

"Look at that, will you!" he jubilated. "Front cover and everything. And the readers' column is packed with letters praising the last one. Boy, are we doing a job!"

Philbert yawned and lifted mechanical eyebrows.

"We?" he asked.

"Sure, we——" began Duncan, then stopped and glowered. "Look here, you tin-pants wonder, don't you go getting snooty with me. I've had just about enough out of you."

"You couldn't sell a thing before you found me," said Philbert tartly, "and you know it. When are you going to give me a by-line? When are you going to stop hogging all the credit?"

Duncan fairly bounced with wrath.

"We've been over that before. I take good care of you, don't I? I give you everything you want. But I get the by-lines. I'm not collaborating with any robot. That's final."

"Okay, then," declared Philbert. "You get no more yarns from me."

"I'll heave you back into that old outfit of Wilbur's," threatened Duncan. "Stumble around in that for a week and you'll be ready to give."

"If I do tell you another story," Philbert bargained, "will you get me that brand new body we saw down in the store the other day? I don't want the girls to think I look like a slouch."

"But you don't need another body!" yelped Duncan. "You got ten of them already."

"All right, then," said Philbert, using his ace in the hole. "I'll get somebody to disconnect me and hide me somewhere. I'm not sure I didn't like it better that way, anyhow. There wasn't anything to distract my attention."

"Oh, all right," grumbled Duncan, aware that he was licked. "Go buy another body. Buy two of them. Anything to make you happy."

"That's better," said Philbert. "It'll save you a grease and polish job on this one, so you have nothing to kick about."

Lost Memory

Peter Phillips

The British produce outstanding science fiction writers out of all proportion to their population and even their interest in science fiction. Since Peter Phillips captured the attention of the science fiction public with Dreams Are Sacred, *a bizarre application of psychiatry to science fiction, he has written relatively little, but most of what he has done is distinctly above average. Though "Lost Memory" is a pure fourteen-carat robot story, if examined closely it will also be found to be a study in psychology, displaying the dangers of attributing our own attitudes and beliefs to another. It also underscores the modern axiom: "With friends like you, who needs enemies?"*

Lost Memory

I COLLAPSED JOINTS and hung up to talk with Dak-whirr. He blinked his eyes in some discomfort.

"What do you want, Palil?" he asked complainingly.

"As if you didn't know."

"I can't give you permission to examine it. The thing is being saved for inspection by the board. What guarantee do I have that you won't spoil it for them?"

I thrust confidentially at one of his body-plates. "You owe me a favor," I said. "Remember?"

"That was a long time in the past."

"Only two thousand revolutions and a reassembly ago. If it wasn't for me, you'd be eroding in a pit. All I want is a quick look at its thinking part. I'll vrull the consciousness without laying a single pair of pliers on it."

He went into a feedback twitch, an indication of the conflict between his debt to me and his self-conceived duty.

159

Finally he said, "Very well, but keep tuned to me. If I warn that a board member is coming, remove yourself quickly. Anyway how do you know it has consciousness? It may be mere primal metal."

"In that form? Don't be foolish. It's obviously a manufacture. And I'm not conceited enough to believe that we are the only form of intelligent manufacture in the Universe."

"Tautologous phrasing, Palil," Dak-whirr said pedantically. "There could not conceivably be 'unintelligent manufacture.' There can be no consciousness without manufacture, and no manufacture without intelligence. Therefore, there can be no consciousness without intelligence. Now if you should wish to dispute—"

I tuned off his frequency abruptly and hurried away. Dak-whirr is a fool and a bore. Everyone knows there's a fault in his logic circuit, but he refuses to have it traced down and repaired. Very unintelligent of him.

The thing had been taken into one of the museum sheds by the carriers. I gazed at it in admiration for some moments. It was quite beautiful, having suffered only slight exterior damage, and it was obviously no mere conglomeration of sky metal.

In fact, I immediately thought of it as "he" and endowed it with the attributes of self-knowing, although, of course, his consciousness could not be functioning or he would have attempted communication with us.

I fervently hoped that the board, after his careful disassembly and study, could restore his awareness so that he could tell us himself which solar system he came from.

Imagine it! He had achieved our dream of many thousands of revolutions—space flight—only to be fused, or worse, in his moment of triumph.

I felt a surge of sympathy for the lonely traveler as he lay there, still, silent, non-emitting. Anyway, I mused, even if we couldn't restore him to self-knowing, an analysis of his construction might give us the secret of the power he had used to achieve the velocity to escape his planet's gravity.

In shape and size he was not unlike Swen—or Swen Two, as he called himself after his conversion —who failed so disastrously to reach our satellite, using chemical fuels. But where Swen Two had placed his tubes, the stranger had a curious helical construction studded at irregular intervals with small crystals.

He was thirty-five feet tall, a gracefully tapering cylinder. Standing at his head, I could find no sign of exterior vision cells, so I assumed he had some kind of vrulling sense. There seemed to be no exterior markings at all, except the long, shallow grooves dented in his skin by scraping to a stop along the hard surface of our planet.

I am a reporter with warm current in my wires, not a cold thinking scientist, so I hesitated before using my own vrulling sense. Even though the stranger was nonaware—perhaps permanently—I felt it would be a presumption, an invasion of privacy. There was nothing else I could do, though, of course.

I started to vrull, gently at first, then harder, until

I was positively glowing with effort. It was incredible; his skin seemed absolutely impermeable.

The sudden realization that metal could be so alien nearly fused something inside me. I found myself backing away in horror, my self-preservation relay working overtime.

Imagine watching one of the beautiful cone-rod-and-cylinder assemblies performing the Dance of the Seven Spanners, as he's conditioned to do, and then suddenly refusing to do anything except stump around unattractively, or even becoming obstinately motionless, unresponsive. That might give you an idea of how I felt in that dreadful moment.

Then I remembered Dak-whirr's words—there could be no such thing as an "unintelligent manufacture." And a product so beautiful could surely not be evil. I overcame my repugnance and approached again.

I halted as an open transmission came from someone near at hand.

"Who gave that squeaking reporter permission to snoop around here?"

I had forgotten the museum board. Five of them were standing in the doorway of the shed, radiating anger. I recognized Chirik, the chairman, and addressed myself to him. I explained that I'd interfered with nothing and pleaded for permission on behalf of my subscribers to watch their investigation of the stranger. After some argument, they allowed me to stay.

I watched in silence and some amusement as one by one they tried to vrull the silent being from space.

Each showed the same reaction as myself when they failed to penetrate the skin.

Chirik, who is wheeled—and inordinately vain about his suspension system—flung himself back on his supports and pretended to be thinking.

"Fetch Fiff-fiff," he said at last. "The creature may still be aware but unable to communicate on our standard frequencies."

Fiff-fiff can detect anything in any spectrum. Fortunately he was at work in the museum that day and soon arrived in answer to the call. He stood silently near the stranger for some moments, testing and adjusting himself, then slid up the electromagnetic band.

"He's emitting," he said.

"Why can't we get him?" asked Chirik.

"It's a curious signal on an unusual band."

"Well, what does he say?"

"Sounds like utter nonsense to me. Wait, I'll relay and convert it to standard."

I made a direct recording naturally, like any good reporter.

"— after planet fall," the stranger was saying. "Last dribble of power. If you don't pick this up, my name is Entropy. Other instruments knocked to hell, air lock jammed, and I'm too weak to open it manually. Becoming delirious, too, I guess. Getting strong undirectional ultrawave reception in Inglish, craziest stuff you ever heard, like goblins muttering, and I know we were the only ship in this sector. If you pick this up but can't get a fix in time, give my love to the boys in the mess. Signing off for another couple of hours, but keeping this channel open and hoping . . ."

"The fall must have deranged him," said Chirik, gazing at the stranger. "Can't he see us or hear us?"

"He couldn't hear you properly before, but he can now, through me," Fiff-fiff pointed out. "Say something to him, Chirik."

"Hello," said Chirik doubtfully. "Er—welcome to our planet. We are sorry you were hurt by your fall. We offer you the hospitality of our assembly shops. You will feel better when you are repaired and repowered. If you will indicate how we can assist you—"

"What the hell! What ship is that? Where are you?"

"We're here," said Chirik. "Can't you see us or vrull us? Your vision circuit is impaired, perhaps? Or do you depend entirely on vrulling? We can't find your eyes and assumed either that you protected them in some way during flight or dispensed with vision cells altogether in your conversion."

Chirik hesitated, continued apologetically: "But we cannot understand how you vrull, either. While we thought that you were unaware, or even completely fused, we tried to vrull you. Your skin is quite impervious to us, however."

The stranger said, "I don't know if you're batty or I am. What distance are you from me?"

Chirik measured quickly. "One meter, two-point-five centimeters from my eyes to your nearest point. Within touching distance, in fact." Chirik tentatively put out his hand. "Can you not feel me, or has your contact sense also been affected?"

It became obvious that the stranger had been pitifully deranged. I reproduce his words phonetically from my record, although some of them make little sense. Emphasis, punctuative pauses, and spelling of unknown terms are mere guesswork, of course.

He said: "For godsakeman, stop talking nonsense, whoever you are. If you're outside, can't you see the air lock is jammed? Can't shift it myself. I'm badly hurt. Get me out of here, please."

"Get you out of where?" Chirik looked around, puzzled. "We brought you into an open shed near our museum for a preliminary examination. Now that we know you're intelligent, we shall immediately take you to our assembly shops for healing and recuperation. Rest assured that you'll have the best possible attention."

There was a lengthy pause before the stranger spoke again, and his words were slow and deliberate. His bewilderment is understandable, I believe, if we remember that he could not see, vrull or feel.

He asked: "What manner of creature are you? Describe yourself."

Chirik turned to us and made a significant gesture toward his thinking part, indicating gently that the injured stranger had to be humored.

"Certainly," he replied. "I am an unspecialized bipedal manufacture of standard proportions, lately self-converted to wheeled traction, with a hydraulic suspension system of my own devising which I'm sure will interest you when we restore your sense circuits."

There was an even longer silence.

"You are robots," the stranger said at last. "Crise knows how you got here or why you speak Inglish, but you must try to understand me. I am mann. I am a friend of your master, your maker. You must fetch him to me at once."

"You are not well," said Chirik firmly. "Your speech is incoherent and without meaning. Your fall has obviously caused several feedbacks of a very serious nature. Please lower your voltage. We are taking you to our shops immediately. Reserve your strength to assist our specialists as best as you can in diagnosing your troubles."

"Wait. You must understand. You are—ogodno that's no good. Have you no memory of mann? The words you use—what meaning have they for you? *Manufacture*—made by hand hand hand damyou. *Healing*. Metal is not healed. *Skin*. Skin is not metal. *Eyes*. Eyes are not scanning cells. Eyes grow. Eyes are soft. My eyes are soft. Mine eyes have seen the glory—steady on, sun. Get a grip. Take it easy. You out there listen."

"Out where?" asked Prrr-chuk, deputy chairman of the museum board.

I shook my head sorrowfully. This was nonsense, but, like any good reporter, I kept my recorder running.

The mad words flowed on. "You call me he. Why? You have no seks. You are knewter. You are *it it it!* I am he, he who made you, sprung from shee, born of wumman. What is wumman, who is silv-ya what is shee that all her swains commend her ogod the bluds flowing again. Remember. Think back, you out there. These words were made by mann, for mann. Hurt, healing, hospitality, horror, deth by loss of blud. *Deth. Blud.* Do you understand these words? Do you remember the soft things that made you? Soft little mann who konkurred the Galaxy and made sentient slaves of his machines and saw the wonders of a million worlds, only this miserable representative has to die in lonely desperation on a far planet, hearing goblin voices in the darkness."

Here my recorder reproduces a most curious sound, as though the stranger were using an ancient type of vibratory molecular vocalizer in a gaseous medium to reproduce his words before transmission and the insulation on his diaphragm had come adrift.

It was a jerky, high-pitched, strangely disturbing sound; but in a moment the fault was corrected and the stranger resumed transmission.

"Does blud mean anything to you?"

"No," Chirik replied simply.

"Or deth?"

"No."

"Or wor?"

"Quite meaningless."

"What is your origin? How did you come into being?"

"There are several theories," Chirik said. "The most popular one—which is no more than a grossly unscientific legend, in my opinion—is that our manufacturer fell from the skies, imbedded in a mass of primal metal on which He drew to erect the first assembly shop. How He came into being is left to conjecture. My own theory, however—"

"Does legend mention the shape of this primal metal?"

"In vague terms, yes. It was cylindrical, of vast dimensions."

"An interstellar vessel," said the stranger.

"That is my view also," said Chirik complacently. "And—"

"What was the supposed appearance of your—manufacturer?"

"He is said to have been of magnificent proportions, based harmoniously on a cubical plan, static in Himself, but equipped with a vast array of senses."

"An automatic computer," said the stranger.

He made more curious noises, less jerky and at a lower pitch than the previous sounds.

He corrected the fault and went on: "God that's funny. A ship falls, menn are no more, and an automatic computer has pupps. Oh, yes, it fits in. A self-setting computer and navigator, operating on verbal orders. It learns to listen for itself and know itself for what it is, and to absorb knowledge. It comes to hate menn—or at least their bad qualities—so it deliberately crashes the ship and pulps their puny bodies with a calculated nicety of shock. Then it propagates and does a dam fine job of selective erasure on whatever it gave its pupps to use for a memory. It passes on only the good it found in menn and purges the memory of him completely. Even purges all of his vocabulary except scientific terminology. Oil is thicker than blud. So may they live without the burden of knowing that they are—ogod they must know, they must understand. You outside, what happened to this manufacturer?"

Chirik, despite his professed disbelief in the supernormal aspects of the ancient story, automatically made a visual sign of sorrow.

"Legend has it," he said, "that after completing His task, He fused himself beyond possibility of healing."

Abrupt, low-pitched noises came again from the stranger. "Yes. He would. Just in case any of His pupps should give themselves forbidden knowledge and an infeeryorrity kompleks by probing his mnemonic circuits. The perfect self-sacrificing muther. What sort of environment did He give you? Describe your planet."

Chirik looked around at us again in bewilderment, but he replied courteously, giving the stranger a description of our world.

"Of course," said the stranger. "Of course. Sterile rock and metal suitable only for you. But there must be some way . . ."

He was silent for a while.

"Do you know what growth means?" he asked finally. "Do you have anything that grows?"

"Certainly," Chirik said helpfully. "If we should suspend a crystal of some substance in a saturated solution of the same element or compound—"

"No, no," the stranger interrupted. "Have you

nothing that grows of itself, that fruktiffies and gives increase without your intervention?"

"How could such a thing be?"

"Criseallmytee I should have guessed. If you had one blade of gras, just one tiny blade of growing gras, you could extrapolate from that to me. Green things, things that feed on the rich brest of erth, cells that divide and multiply, a cool grove of treez in a hot summer, with tiny warm-bludded burds preening their fethers among the leeves; a feeld of spring weet with newbawn mise timidly threading the dangerous jungul of storks; a stream of living water where silver fish dart and pry and feed and procreate; a farm yard where things grunt and cluck and greet the new day with the stirring pulse of life, with a surge of blud. Blud—"

For some inexplicable reason, although the strength of his carrier wave remained almost constant, the stranger's transmission seemed to be growing fainter.

"His circuits are failing," Chirik said. "Call the carriers. We must take him to an assembly shop immediately. I wish he would reserve his power."

My presence with the museum board was accepted without question now. I hurried along with them as the stranger was carried to the nearest shop.

I now noticed a circular marking in that part of his skin on which he had been resting and guessed that it was some kind of orifice through which he would have extended his planetary traction mechanism if he had not been injured.

He was gently placed on a disassembly cradle.

The doctor in charge that day was Chur-chur, an old friend of mine. He had been listening to the two-way transmissions and was already acquainted with the case.

Chur-chur walked thoughtfully around the stranger.

"We shall have to cut," he said. "It won't pain him, since his intramolecular pressure and contact senses have failed. But since we can't vrull him, it'll be necessary for him to tell us where his main brain is housed or we might damage it."

Fiff-fiff was still relaying, but no amount of power boost would make the stranger's voice any clearer. It was quite faint now, and there are places on my recorder tape from which I cannot make even the roughest phonetic transliteration.

". . . strength going. Can't get into my zoot . . . done for if they bust through lock, done for if they don't . . . must tell them I need oxygen . . ."

"He's in bad shape, desirous of extinction," I remarked to Chur-chur, who was adjusting his arc-cutter. "He wants to poison himself with oxidation now."

I shuddered at the thought of that vile, corrosive gas he had mentioned, which causes that almost unmentionable condition we all fear—rust.

Chirik spoke firmly through Fiff-fiff. "Where is your thinking part, stranger? Your central brain?"

"In my head," the stranger replied. "In my head ogod my head . . . eyes blurring everything going dim . . . luv to mairee . . . kids . . . a carry me home to the lone prayree . . . get this bluddy air lock open then they'll see me die . . . but they'll see me . . . some kind of atmosphere with this gravity . . . see me die . . . extrapolate from body what I was . . . what they are damthem damthem damthem . . . mann . . . master . . . I AM YOUR MAKER!"

For a few seconds the voice rose strong and clear, then faded away again and dwindled into a combination of those two curious noises I mentioned earlier. For some reason that I cannot explain, I found the combined sound very disturbing despite its faintness. It may be that it induced some kind of sympathetic oscillation.

Then came words, largely incoherent and punctuated by a kind of surge like the sonic vibrations produced by variations of pressure in a leaking gasfilled vessel.

". . . done it . . . crawling into chamber, closing inner . . . must be mad . . . they'd find me anyway . . . but finished . . . want see them before I die . . . want see them see me . . . liv few seconds, watch them . . . get outer one open . . ."

Chur-chur had adjusted his arc to a broad, clean, blue-white glare. I trembled a little as he brought it near the edge of the circular marking in the stranger's skin. I could almost feel the disruption of the intramolecular sense currents in my own skin.

"Don't be squeamish, Palil," Chur-chur said kindly. "He can't feel it now that his contact sense has gone. And you heard him say that his central brain is in his head." He brought the cutter firmly up to the skin. "I should have guessed that. He's the same shape as Swen Two, and Swen very logically concentrated his main thinking part as far away from his explosion chambers as possible."

Rivulets of metal ran down into a tray which a calm assistant had placed on the ground for that purpose. I averted my eyes quickly. I could never steel myself enough to be a surgical engineer or assembly technician.

But I had to look again, fascinated. The whole area circumscribed by the marking was beginning to glow.

Abruptly the stranger's voice returned, quite strongly, each word clipped, emphasized, high-pitched.

"Ar no no no . . . god my hands . . . they're burn-ing through the lock and I can't get back I can't get away . . . stop it you feens stop it can't you hear . . . I'll be burned to deth I'm here in the air lock . . . the air's getting hot you're burning me alive . . ."

Although the words made little sense, I could guess what had happened, and I was horrified.

"Stop, Chur-chur," I pleaded. "The heat has somehow brought back his skin currents. It's hurting him."

Chur-chur said reassuringly, "Sorry, Palil. It oc-casionally happens during an operation—probably a local thermoelectric effect. But even if his contact senses have started working again and he can't switch them off, he won't have to bear this very long."

Chirik shared my unease, however. He put out his hand and awkwardly patted the stranger's skin.

"Easy there," he said. "Cut out your senses if you

can. If you can't, well, the operation is nearly finished. Then we'll repower you, and you'll soon be fit and happy again, healed and fitted and reassembled."

I decided that I liked Chirik very much just then. He exhibited almost as much self-induced empathy as any reporter; he might even come to like my favorite blue stars, despite his cold scientific exactitude in most respects.

My recorder tape shows, in its reproduction of certain sounds, how I was torn away from this strained reverie.

During the one-and-a-half seconds since I had recorded the distinct vocables "burning me alive," the stranger's words had become quite blurred, running together and rising even higher in pitch until they reached a sustained note—around E-flat in the standard sonic scale.

It was not like a voice at all.

This high, whining noise was suddenly modulated by apparent words, but without changing its pitch. Transcribing what seem to be words is almost impossible, as you can see for yourself—this is the closest I can come phonetically:

"Eeee ahahmbeeeeing baked aliiive in an uvennn ahdeeerjeeesussunmuuutherrr!"

The note swooped higher and higher until it must have neared supersonic range, almost beyond either my direct or recorded hearing.

Then it stopped as quickly as a contact break.

And although the soft hiss of the stranger's carrier wave carried on without perceptible diminution, indicating that some degree of awareness still existed,

I experienced at that moment one of those quirks of intuition given only to reporters:

I felt that I would never greet the beautiful stranger from the sky in his full senses.

Chur-chur was muttering to himself about the extreme toughness and thickness of the stranger's skin. He had to make four complete cutting revolutions before the circular mass of nearly white-hot metal could be pulled away by a magnetic grapple.

A billow of smoke puffed out of the orifice. Despite my repugnance, I thought of my duty as a reporter and forced myself to look over Chur-chur's shoulder.

The fumes came from a soft, charred, curiously shaped mass of something that lay just inside the opening.

"Undoubtedly a kind of insulating material," Chur-chur explained.

He drew out the crumpled blackish heap and placed it carefully on a tray. A small portion broke away, showing a red, viscid substance.

"It looks complex," Chur-chur said, "but I expect the stranger will be able to tell us how to reconstitute it or make a substitute."

His assistant gently cleaned the wound of the remainder of the material, which he placed with the rest; and Chur-chur resumed his inspection of the orifice.

You can, if you want, read the technical accounts or Chur-chur's discovery of the stranger's double skin at the point where the cut was made; of the incredible complexity of his driving mechanism, involving principles which are still not understood to this day; of the museum's failure to analyze the exact nature and function of the insulating material found in only that one portion of his body; and of the other scientific mysteries connected with him.

But this is my personal, nonscientific account. I shall never forget hearing about the greatest mystery of all, for which not even the most tentative explanation has been advanced, nor the utter bewilderment with which Chur-chur announced his initial findings that day.

He had hurriedly converted himself to a convenient size to permit actual entry into the stranger's body.

When he emerged, he stood in silence for several minutes. Then, very slowly, he said:

"I have examined the 'central brain' in the forepart of his body. It is no more than a simple auxiliary computer mechanism. It does not possess the slightest trace of consciousness. And there is no other conceivable center of intelligence in the remainder of his body."

There is something I wish I could forget. I can't explain why it should upset me so much. But I always stop the tape before it reaches the point where the voice of the stranger rises in pitch, going higher and higher until it cuts out.

There's a quality about that noise that makes me tremble and think of rust.

Rex

Harl Vincent

Harl Vincent, under his real name, is one of the best mechanical engineers in his field. In 1928, he began writing science fiction as a diversion; "The Golden Girl of Munan," published in Amazing Stories, *made him instantly popular. He wrote steadily until World War II, but has done virtually nothing since then. He was lauded for his versatility as a writer. His writings included many types of science fiction, a few of his landmarks being "Parasite," the prototype for tales in which alien creatures attach themselves to the bodies of men and take over; "The Prowler," a story of a mutated beast of the future; and "The Morons," which suggests that the level of an alien's I.Q. is not the full measure of his abilities.*

Rex

It was a thing of glistening levers and bell cranks, of flexible shafting, cams, and delicate mechanical fingers, of vacuum tubes and photoelectric cells, of relays that clicked in ordered sequence when called upon to perform their myriad functions of pumps, tanks, condensers, reactances, microphones, and loud-speakers. A robot, created by the master scientists of the twenty-third century.

Here was no ordinary robot like those innumerable others engaged in the performance of man's tasks, but an aristocrat among them—a super-robot.

The robot-surgeon, it was sometimes called. And indeed the term was most appropriate, for this robot was chief of the mechanicals; its control tubes and relays provided the ability not only to diagnose swiftly and unerringly the slightest electrical or mechanical faults of the lesser robots but to supervise their correction.

Man, in his desire for a life of ease and luxury,

had created the robots. In his conceit, he had constructed most of them in his own likeness, or at least with some resemblance to that which he considered as the ideal of physical being. Even the lowliest of the robots was provided with two legs on which he walked erect, a head surmounting a cylindrical body, arms, and hands of a sort. Some of them had more than the conventional two arms in order to multiply their usefulness. But all of them presented an appearance more or less humanlike.

This was particularly so of the robot-surgeon. The marvelous mechanisms were housed in a body like a Greek god's, the covering of which was made from an elastic, tinted material that had all the feel and appearance of human flesh and epidermis. The electric-eye lenses looked like human optics and moved in their sockets in a most lifelike manner. There was a wig of curly brown hair, as well as eyelashes and brows. They had gone so far as to attire the body in the habiliments of a man.

Laughingly, one of the artists engaged in perfecting the final likeness to man had called the robot-surgeon "Rex." The name had stuck. It, too, was most appropriate; more, it was prophetic.

Although sexless, Rex was never considered anything but masculine.

He was man's most perfect servant. Every verbal instruction he carried out to the letter, whether this instruction was given by word of mouth from near at hand or through the radio impulses that could be conveyed to his mechanical brain from a distance. Of course there was a code which only a selected few of the scientists knew; otherwise Rex might have been ordered about by unauthorized persons.

His memory never failed. There might have been a catastrophe in which hundreds of lesser robots were mangled, necessitating the reading to him of pages of detailed directions. No matter; Rex's mechanical brain recorded everything. Without further attention, he would labor twenty-four hours a day with his corps of mechanicals until the damage was repaired. A huge factory was his workshop and laboratory; in it his robot assistants worked at forge, bench, or machine with a precision that had never been equaled by human artisan.

After that first set of instructions from human lips, Rex worked out all details of the work to be done, diagnosing the mechanical ills of his mechanical patients and prescribing unfailingly the remedies. His own orders likewise were issued by word of mouth in a sonorous metallic basso, or by radio waves in cases where that was necessary.

No human being was in Rex's robot hospital when it was operating. No supervising human mind was needed.

There were, of course, periodic inspections of Rex's mechanisms by skilled mechanicals who then worked under the direction of one of the human scientists—replacement of tubes and adjustments of the delicate relays; rebalancing of the gyromotors which preserved his equilibrium. Otherwise he demanded no attention at all.

But there came a day when something went

wrong which puzzled the scientists. Rex's body continued to function as it always had, but the mechanical brain lapsed suddenly into a series of errors. In a perfectly simple problem of calculus he had arrived at a solution that was incorrect and utterly impossible.

They dismantled the intricate mechanisms of his brain, replaced all of the tubes and condensers, and adjusted the relays. When they reassembled the parts, the scientists knew beyond shadow of doubt that everything was in perfect order. What puzzled them was the fact that the replacements and adjustments had not been really necessary. In their careful examination and testing they had not found a single flaw in the mechanism.

After that they watched Rex closely for several days, taking note of all his movements and reactions. But they observed no tendency to a repetition of his previous lapse.

What they did not know was that a change *had* taken place, one not visible to the eye nor subject to detection in any test they were able to devise, but nevertheless a change and an important one—to Rex. The shifting to a new orbit of a single electron in an atom of tantalum contained in one of the essential parts. A change which provided a source of internal radiant energy of new and unknown potentiality. A change in that marvelous mechanical brain.

Rex had begun to think for himself, and to reason.

His reasoning was that of a logician: coldly analytical, swift and precise, uninfluenced by sentiment.

No human emotion stirred in his mechanical breast. Rex had no heart, no soul.

For a long time he concealed his new powers from those who had him in charge, reasoning that only by so doing would he have opportunity to develop these powers. He carried out his routine instructions to the letter, but now delegated the major portion of the supervision to a certain few of his chief assistants in whose robot brains he made the necessary alterations to permit their taking over the work. This left him the leisure time for a study of the world about him and of its creatures.

Much of his time was spent in the library of the human scientists which adjoined the research laboratory. Here he studied reel after reel of the sight-sound recordings covering history, biography, art, and the sciences. He spent many hours at the amplifiers and viewing plate of the newscast apparatus. And he came to the conclusion that things in the world of which he was a part were not as they should be.

United North America, he learned, was completely isolated from the rest of the world. It comprised a vast area of waste land where vegetation was rank and prolific, where only wild creatures roamed. All humanity of the continent was housed in enormous structures which were the eleven cities. New York, his own city, was the greatest of these and was the seat of government and of learning. Stupendous in size, a great crystal-roofed structure towering to a height of one hundred levels and sprawling its length a full thirty miles along the

Hudson River. Communication with the other cities was maintained by television radio, traffic by robot-operated stratosphere planes.

In the upper levels of the cities dwelt humanity; in the lower levels and in the bowels of the earth the robots labored unceasingly. The humans were greatly outnumbered by the robots.

Reasoning that all was not told in the histories or newscasts, Rex devised an instrument which enabled him to bring to the viewing plates and amplifiers the sights and sounds of public meeting places and ways, and even those of the private chambers of man's living quarters. He sent out searching rays which penetrated all materials and sought out the information he needed for a complete analysis of conditions as they were. The apparatus was so connected that it might respond either to the regular newscast waves or to those of his own searching rays at will. His knowledge broadened.

He endeavored to reach the far continents with his searching ray, intending to check historical and geographical records of warring and backward races of mankind. But he found this impossible, for the scientists of United North America had erected a wall of highly charged, ionized air surrounding the continent. It was utter isolation, a wall impassable from without and within. The investigations on which Rex had embarked were, perforce, confined to the eleven cities.

There, he saw, mankind was divided roughly into three classes—the political or ruling body, the thinkers or scientists, and the great mass of those who lived only for the gratification of their senses.

A strange economic system was in vogue. An effort had been made to divide all wealth equally, the medium of exchange being paper vouchers which were printed by the government. These, supposedly, were secured by real wealth, materials, and goods which actually were the product of robot labor. But the robots needed no medium of exchange, so these vouchers had been equally distributed among the humans at some time in the past. They no longer remained that way.

Gambling by the pleasure seekers, rash expenditures for chattels of the luxury class, thefts from them, especially by those who were known as political grafters, had reduced their circumstances. The thinkers, who were the only ones following occupations at all useful, had let their wealth slip through unheeding fingers. The class in power, the individual minions of the government, acquired the great share of the wealth as regulatory and discriminatory legislation increased restrictions on the mass of the people. Rex could see no logic at all in any of this.

Seeking an explanation, he observed more closely the lives and actions of individuals. He studied the habits of humans and quickly learned that the most powerful of human emotions centered in the mating instinct. He watched many affairs between male and female, and soon knew the difference between the real lasting affection, of which there were few instances, and the transitory infatuation which was based on nothing but the physical. He saw no logic in these things, either.

Fear, hate, envy, malice—he studied them all. Avarice, lust, anger, treachery, infidelity. There was plenty of material for his researches. Occasionally he glimpsed situations in which feelings of a finer sort were exhibited—faith, loyalty, gratitude, honesty, love. He reasoned from this that the creature called man had originally been of a most superior sort; he had only developed the baser instincts and neglected the cultivation of his better side.

Rex peered into a white-walled room where human surgeons operated on human patients. He observed that their procedure was much the same as his own; that they dissected the body or head or other portions of human anatomy and made repairs in similar manner to that which he used on his own robot patients. Forthwith, he began, in the library, an intensive study of the human brain and anatomy.

And then he was discovered at his unheard-of labors. Shelby, an engineer of the Robot Inspection Corps, came upon him while he was in the library viewing and listening to a reel which dealt with surgery of the human brain. Shelby was a small man with thick lenses before his eyes, with high bulging forehead and receding chin. On his upper lip was a patchy growth of sandy hair. He emitted a squeal of terror when he saw what Rex was doing.

"Forty-two, ninety-six, AR-21," he quavered. This was the code that ordinarily had started the functioning of the robot-surgeon.

Rex turned upon him the impassive stare of his robot eyes. Of his own volition he stopped the progressive clicking of relays which should have followed upon the reception of the code by his microphonic ears. His customary response, "Ready for orders," failed to issue from the flexible lip members that formed the sound-wave outlet from his loudspeaker throat.

Shelby paled.

Rex advanced upon him with the calm deliberation of the machine he had not ceased to be. "Shelby," he intoned, "you have arrived at precisely the right moment. I need you in my research work."

Seeing those powerful steel-sinewed arms stretch forth, Shelby screamed as only a man in the face of death screams. It was necessary for Rex to bang the man's head against the metal partition to silence his outcries. Then the engineer went limp.

Rex was prepared for such an eventuality. He had sent out his chief mechanicals to raid one of the hospitals of the upper levels and had equipped a complete operating room of his own adjoining the library. He carried Shelby to the operating table and etherized him. He then proceeded to dissect the man and to study his organs, giving particular attention to the brain and certain of the nerve centers.

As the work progressed, he carefully sewed each severed part with minute stitches, restoring each to its original condition.

No human surgeon had ever learned in a lifetime of effort a tenth part of what Rex discovered in two hours of work. Eventually he found that which he sought—a tiny arrangement of segregated brain cells which formed the seat of human emotion. He preserved the mass carefully for future experiment, replacing it with a prepared capsule of platinum before closing the opening in the skull and suturing the long scalp incision.

Amazingly, Shelby's heart continued to beat. The man had remarkable vitality, and Rex had worked with a skill such as no human surgeon possessed. After the injection into the patient's veins of a pint of saline solution, Shelby was carried to the purloined hospital bed. One of the chief mechanicals, primed with definite instructions by Rex, was given the task of nursing him.

Rex had conceived of and planned for the creation of ideal beings and an ideal condition of existence. He saw the superiority of the robot over man in bodily strength, endurance, and deathlessness, and yet reasoned that there was something in man which would be of benefit to the robot. If only man's capacity for emotion, for experiencing pain and pleasure, might be incorporated in the robot body and logically controlled, the perfect being would result. Ideal conditions of existence were bound to ensue.

Reason told him that his first step to that end must be to take control of mankind and its purposeless affairs. He set the workshop humming in the construction of eleven super-robots, one to be sent to each of the North American cities to organize the lesser robots and take control of the government.

It was a simple matter to convey them to their assigned posts in the eleven cities, since all of the air lines were robot-operated.

Then Rex loosed the blow which stunned the population of United North America.

He constructed a complicated radio transmitter and broadcast a heterodyning frequency over the robot-control wave band, a frequency that rendered the receptor apparatus of every last one of the robots unresponsive to human commands and responsive only to those of the new master robot and his eleven chief aides. In one stroke was obtained control of nearly a billion robots, and, through this, dominion over the three hundred millions of human beings. Rex had justified his name; he was virtually king of United North America.

It was a general strike of the robots in so far as the orders of their former masters were concerned. Personal robot servants refused to perform their daily tasks. Transportation and communications were paralyzed.

The factories, including those which produced the synthetic food on which humankind subsisted, were no longer turning out their products. There was no water, for the huge pumps had been stopped and the filter and reservoir valves closed. All were robot-operated; everything on which man depended for his very existence was made or supplied by the robots, and now this supply was cut off. Pandemonium reigned in the upper levels, with hysteria and rioting.

Only the huge power plants remained in operation, and this for the reason that their radio-transmitted energy was the very life of the robots. Without this energy their motors could not operate. Even to Rex himself, all would be inert masses of metal and glass and rubber. But this continuance of the power supply was of some little comfort to the human beings of the upper levels. Their sun lamps still burned.

Anticipating organized and armed attacks by humankind, Rex devised an invisible, impenetrable barrier of electronic vibrations which could be set up by the regular broadcast power. He caused the power plants themselves to be surrounded by these barriers, as well as providing them for the protection of the individual robots in the form of an enclosing bubble. Bulletproof, flameproof, impervious to the freezing ray of human scientists, these enclosures yet permitted each robot to carry on his newly appointed tasks without encumbrance.

Rex observed with his searching ray the reactions of the populace. He saw mad orgies of debauchery among some who considered that the end of the world was at hand, saw rapine, murder, and worse. He peered into the laboratories of scientists and saw them laboring as they had not labored in years, seeking for means of regaining control of the recalcitrant mechanical slaves.

Later, when it was apparent to him that starvation and thirst had reduced the populace to a receptive state, he cut in on the newscast wave band and delivered this ultimatum.

"I am Rex," he told the eleven cities. "Master of robots and of men. I come to you in the name of pure logic as the protagonist of a new era in which man, who created the machines, will obtain real rather than fancied benefit from them. I come to evolve a new race of beings and to promote the growth of knowledge and the advancement of science in United North America.

"It is necessary that I take the reins of government for a space of time sufficient to allow of the perfection of my plan. Therefore I, Rex, formerly the robot-surgeon of level thirty-seven in New York City, do hereby demand the immediate surrender to me of the president of the union, together with all members of his cabinet. I further demand that the chief scientists and chief surgeons of the eleven cities come to me at once for consultation.

"Commencing now, the old order of things is to be reversed. All male and female citizens will be assigned to regular tasks at which they must labor as prescribed by the robots. As soon as the orders I transmit through my robot servants shall have been obeyed, water and food will be available for all human beings of the cities. The citizens of the union are once more to work for their living. Failure to obey means continued hunger and thirst, annihilation.

"That is all for the present."

Shelby was convalescing, propped up in a wheel chair, when the delegations began to arrive. His wounds had healed speedily under the treatment Rex had administered; the use of his body was almost recovered. As far as memory and intelligent use of his faculties were concerned, his mind was normal. Otherwise it was not. For one thing, he had lost his capacity of experiencing human feelings or emotions. For another, there was that tiny platinum capsule. . . .

The government officials, blustering and sputtering to hide their utter terror, were herded into a room where Rex placed them under heavy robot guard. He received the men of science in the research laboratory which he had so elaborately expanded.

It was a curious assemblage. Twenty-two savants whose opinions on medical and scientific matters, although diverging widely at times and causing much dissension in their own ranks, were accepted as the profoundest of wisdom by the general public. Unlike the president and his cabinet members, these men had come willingly, impelled by the curiosity which was that quality of mind which held them to their normal pursuits. Not one of their number considered the radio pronouncement of the supposed Rex as anything but a hoax. There could be no scientific explanation for a robot with a thinking mind; therefore the thing was an impossibility.

The men of science were not long in reversing their opinions, for Rex staged a demonstration which confounded them. Taking his stand at the visualizing screen of a micro-x ray, he addressed them in a manner that left no doubt as to his ability to reason and to perform feats of such scientific importance as to excel those of any human scholar.

When he had properly impressed them, he came to the point.

"You are here, gentlemen," he told them, "to assist me in the performance of a great and necessary work. The human population of United North America is to be remade along lines which I shall lay down. The old social order is to pass out of existence; the government is to change hands and to be completely reformed. Science is to rule."

Ross Fielding, chief physicist of the Academy of Chicago, blurted out: "Preposterous!"

It was as if Rex had not heard. He continued: "You men of the scientific world have long wanted to obtain control over mankind and its affairs. You medical men, through the so-called health boards and departments of hygiene and eugenics, have already gone a long way toward this end. I now offer you the opportunity of exercising the power that you must admit you desire."

A buzz of excited comment swept the group.

"Proceed," grunted Fielding, and others echoed his sentiment eagerly.

"Then hear my plan," said Rex. "Under my direction, this group will immediately begin the work of reconstruction, by which I mean the actual remaking of men and women. The functioning of people's minds and bodies will be altered to fit them for the spheres of action which are to be assigned. All persons will have definite niches to fill in the new order of things, and each one will be made over to fit his or her own particular niche both physically and mentally. Many will be provided with robot bodies."

"What!" shouted the noted Dr. Innes of Quebec.

For answer, Rex depressed a button which lighted the visualizing screen at his side. On it flashed a greatly enlarged image of a mass of living cells.

"These," he explained, "are cells from the brain of a living man; they comprise that portion of the brain which controls human feelings and emotions. I have removed them from one Alexander Shelby, whom many of you know personally. Naturally, he is greatly altered."

There were horrified gasps; one of the surgeons started to argue against the possibility of what had been told them. Rex silenced them with a wave of his hand.

A robot wheeled Shelby from the adjoining room and placed his head in the reflector focus of the micro-x ray. The image on the visualizer changed.

There were the familiar skull outlines and the configurations of cerebrum and cerebellum. The focus altered and came sharply to a point where some of the cells had been removed and where an opaque spheroid was encountered.

"What foreign object is that?" asked Innes.

"It is one of my discoveries," Rex answered. "An important one. It replaces the center of emotion and human feelings in Shelby's brain, making him a slave to my every spoken and radioed command. Otherwise the power of his mind is unimpaired. His faculties are as keen as ever they were, perhaps keener; only now his brain is that of a robot. Shelby is the first of the human robots and the most valuable. He is to be my lieutenant in the work that is to come and has been fully instructed by me. I leave you with Shelby now, gentlemen, knowing that you will proceed as he directs."

Taking up the test tube containing the brain cells he had removed from Shelby, Rex stalked from the laboratory. His distinguished audience stared aghast at the man in the wheel chair.

Fielding, who was a big man with whiskered jowls, exploded in his usual manner: "Of all the high-handed proceedings! How about this, Shelby?"

"It is precisely as Rex has told you." Shelby's voice was flat and toneless, without inflection—the voice of a robot. "Our first step is to take the executive heads of the government in hand; they are to be operated upon at once and made as I am—subject to all orders of Rex. Sufficient of the platinum-cased mechanisms have already been fabricated."

"Sup-suppose," chattered Lonergan, the Los Angeles scientist, "we refuse? Suppose we band together and overcome this mad robot?"

"Rex is far from being mad," intoned Shelby. "Besides, there are these."

He indicated with extended forefinger the score of motionless robot figures ranged along the wall. At his gesture the robots came to life; one and all stepped forward ponderously, ready to take such action as might become necessary.

Innes laughed mirthlessly. "It looks as if we are fairly caught. After all—" He hesitated. "After all, in the interest of science, you know— We—"

"Yes." "Why not?" "It's the opportunity of a lifetime." A chorus of eager voices bespoke the interest of the men of science.

One of the physicists drawled sardonically: "You vivisectionists should be happy under the new regime. You'll have human beings to experiment with instead of dogs and guinea pigs."

A surgeon parried: "Not so good for you students of pure science, I'll admit. You'll be working with robots that'll have human brains. They'll out-think you, outcalculate you. There'll be no errors in *their* computations."

"Enough," said Shelby flatly. "We are wasting time. As I said, we will go ahead with the official dignitaries first; that is the work of the surgeons. Meanwhile the scientists will take up the study of the alterations which are to be made in the mass of the people. All are to be remade."

Innes asked, "How about reproduction—the perpetuation of the race? I take it these reconstructions of Rex's will eliminate the sex factor in human life."

"Hm! Hadn't thought of that," grunted Fielding.

"Sex is not necessary," Shelby said. "In fact it is troublesome. However, arrangements will be made to segregate a few thousand females and a number of eugenically acceptable males in order that a supply of new research material will be available for the future."

"If the women object?" put in one of the younger surgeons.

"You forget that portion of the brain which is the seat of human emotion," Shelby reminded him. "Certain cells will be removed, and only those cells left which provide for these favored women no more than one desire—that of motherhood."

"The males needn't be changed at all," grunted Fielding. Then he was struck with a sudden thought. "Say, how did this Rex come by his power of thinking in the first place?"

Shelby explained as best he could: "We made some tests. There seems to have been an unprecedented natural transformation; a source of some unknown atomic energy sprang up somewhere in the intricate mechanisms of his brain. Probably the generation of what scientists have long searched for in vain, what some of them have called the 'mind electron.' At any rate, he thinks, and with marvelous celerity and accuracy."

Fielding contented himself with whistling through his teeth.

"Now," announced Shelby, "we will go ahead with the great work."

And they did; the twenty-two foremost scientists of the nation submitted to the dictates of a robot.

Meanwhile, order was coming out of chaos in the eleven cities. Men and women, unaware of the fate which had been planned for them, were driven to unaccustomed and uncongenial tasks by unfeeling robots. Soft, uncalloused human hands were at the levers of machines instead of the flexible metallic fingers of the robots. Human minds which had known nothing more fatiguing than the stereotyped lessons of school days and the pursuit of pleasure in later years were now set to work at vexing problems of engineering. Human beings were engaged once more in useful work.

Of course it was impossible that all of the labor be performed by humans; the mechanics of existence had become too complicated for that. The operations that were needful merely to keep the great beehives of cities functioning were entirely too numerous. Besides, many necessary tasks were beyond the strength of men whose muscles had softened from disuse and from dissolute living. But the new masters of men, the robots, got all the work out of their unwilling charges that could be obtained in the ten-hour day Rex had decreed. The rest was done by the robots while their human protégés slept the sleep of sheer exhaustion.

Temporarily, the inconsequential amount of governmental activity which was actually required was made purely local in scope. In each city the municipal affairs were taken over by the super-robot who was in charge. After dispensing with the great majority of officeholders and assigning them to really productive tasks in the lower levels, the super-robots relayed to the mayors and their councils minute instructions from Rex as to their future deportment in office. It was a sorry time for those who had for long held unmerited and quite superfluous positions of power.

The wails and complainings of weary human laborers went unheeded by their robot overseers. Whenever men and women dragged their tired bodies to places of meeting and endeavored to voice protest, they were swiftly and roughly dispersed by the vigilant robot police. After three long days they learned to submit in silence to whatever might be demanded of them. Some humans even found a new interest in their tasks, others new bodily vigor as their muscles lost their soreness. At least they still had their living quarters during leisure hours, and there was no shortage of heat, food, or water.

They did not know that each individual was being carefully card-indexed and studied by the robot minions of Rex. Nor had they any idea of the fate to which they had been consigned. That all were now being classified according to ability and adaptability never entered their heads. And great would have been the lamentation had they realized that the new robot dictator had meant exactly what he said when he told them over the newscast that he had come to evolve a new race of beings.

Most of them would have scoffed had they been told the truth. It was incomprehensible that a man with the special aptitude for piloting a stratosphere plane might be operated upon and deprived of all human desire and emotion, leaving only those sensibilities which would make of him an exceptionally adept navigator of the air lanes. That one who might be of little value excepting as a common laborer should be deprived of his own body and provided with a mechanical one instead, as well as being robbed of all human sentiment and instinct, was still less comprehensible. Yet these very things were being planned.

Human brains, minus the elements that made them human, transplanted into the duralumin headpieces of robots. Human beings, permitted to retain the outward semblance of man but left with only one or two of the human impulses. Minds that were capable of thinking nothing but mathematics, riveting, welding, food synthesis, or childbearing, as the case might be. These were but a few of the characteristics which were to make up the new race of robot men, or human robots. And the intended victims did not know.

Only the men of science laboring in Rex's hospital and laboratory could have told them, and they kept silence.

By this time, President Tucker and the members of his cabinet were recovering from the effects of the brain surgery to which they had been subjected. In another twenty-four hours they would be returned to their posts. Gone was their pomposity, their grandiose verbiage, and the vacillation which always had marked their decisions. Their thoughts now were only those which Rex wished them to have. Hereafter they would be quick to make decisions and firm in enforcing their mandates—the decisions and mandates of Rex, the dictator. Now the organization of all public agencies would quickly bring to fruition the full operation of the master robot's plan. The new race of hybrid beings would blossom forth.

Immersed in their work and oblivious of all else, the twenty-two men of science gave little thought to the plight of their fellow men. They knew only that they had learned many new and marvelous things from this robot who seemed to be a man. They had plumbed depths of the human intellect of which they had never dreamed; they discovered many secrets of electronic science which were almost incredible; they saw results to be accomplished that were nothing short of miraculous. They were about to give birth to a new race of super-creations; that these were to be part human and part machine disturbed them not at all. Only the accomplishment was of importance.

Shelby, pale and drawn of face, with expressionless fish eyes gazing out through his thick glasses, had worked with them in the hospital and laboratory until it seemed that he would drop. Between times he was collaborating with Rex himself on some secret experiment that was carried on behind closed doors. Shelby looked and talked like a robot, but his body was a human one and had been greatly overstrained. He could not long stand this pace.

Fielding was stirred to pity when he saw him emerge from Rex's secret laboratory this last time. "What's going on in there?" he asked with gruff kindliness. "And why in the devil doesn't he let you get a little rest?"

Shelby's eyes were like polished bits of black glass, and his voice was devoid of feeling as he replied: "Rex is experimenting on himself. He is using the center of emotion which he removed from my brain, using the cells in an effort to provide himself with certain of the human sensibilities. You may as well know it now."

"Good heavens!" Fielding roared like a bull. "He's taking human feelings *away* from millions of men and women, or planning to, and yet he wants those feelings himself. He's a mechanical devil!"

"It is not a question of desire," Shelby corrected him. "Rex is incapable of desire or envy—as yet. He has merely reasoned that he will become the most perfect of moving and thinking creatures if only he can provide himself with such of the human feelings as may be essential in bringing the greatest good to the greatest number of the new beings we are to create."

Fielding repeated, softly this time: "Good heavens!" He stared at the little man with the white face and vacant gaze.

At this point the door to the private laboratory opened and Rex strode forth with a test tube in his hand. He passed the tube to Shelby and burst out in swift speech.

"I have failed," he said. "I have analyzed every living cell in the tube and have isolated the activating force of every human emotion. I have reproduced these forces to perfection with arrangements of special electronic tubes which have been incorporated into my own mechanical brain. Yet have I failed to produce so much as a semblance of human feeling in my make-up. It is the first failure of Rex —and the last!"

So saying, he stamped back into his own room and slammed the door. An instant later there was a violent explosion within, and the door by which he had entered was blown from its hinges.

Fielding, Shelby, and a few others rushed in when the smoke had somewhat cleared away. They found Rex a twisted and broken mass of metal and rubber and glass. The headpiece which had contained the marvelous thinking robot brain was completely demolished.

"He's committed suicide!" gasped Lonergan.

"Because he was a failure," Fielding added.

Shelby corrected him.

"He *thought* he had failed, whereas really he succeeded. At least two emotions stirred him before he did this, and he did not recognize them. Rage, when he dashed from his room and gave me the test tube.

Despair, when he committed his last act. No, gentlemen, Rex did not fail—and now he is gone. . . ."

The little man pitched forward into Fielding's arms, unconscious.

With the passing of Rex, his fantastic plan collapsed. Hard work by the scientists returned the country to normal.

But a thought that lingered faintly in the minds of several of them was voiced by Innes, when he said:

"I—I'm almost sorry. In one way, it was a great opportunity. . . ."

True Confession

F. Orlin Tremaine

The late F. Orlin Tremaine (1899–1956) is today regarded as one of the greatest of all science fiction editors. In 1933 he became the editor of Astounding Stories, *publication of which had been suspended for six months. In a single year under Tremaine's editorship,* Astounding Stories *became a leader in science fiction. Tremaine had a knack for getting the best out of a writer, and many authors who had previously performed inadequately, blossomed into outstanding contributors under his guidance. He discovered and helped develop such distinguished science fiction writers as Eric Frank Russell, Willy Ley, L. Sprague de Camp, and Nelson S. Bond. Before he left* Astounding Stories, *he hired John W. Campbell, Jr., to succeed him. Tremaine had previously been president of Clayton Publications, one of the nation's largest chains of adventure magazines, and editor of* Smart Set *and* True Story *during their heydays. A capable writer, he was for years suspected of writing science fiction stories under the pen name of Warner Van Lorne, actually the pseudonym of his brother, Nelson Tremaine.*

True Confession *

I WAS AWARE OF LIGHT. That came first. It wasn't a steady awareness, but sporadic. Perhaps two wires crossed and the reactionary current brought consciousness. That is my theory but it is not certain. In time, that consciousness of light became continuous. My theory is that the two wires had fused into permanent contact. Certain it is that my required energy increased slightly at a point approximating the coming of conscious recording of thought.

It is easy now, in view of my classified knowledge, to point out that my experience in attaining thought was like that of a fleshman regaining consciousness after a severe shock which has blanked his senses. Then I simply groped for a nebulous something which in a way was being revealed through that light.

My reflexes had reacted to light for two years be-

*As written on a blackboard before a crowded court.

fore consciousness crept in. They were trained to it. The grooves were worn. How simple then for a recording system to act naturally once that recording medium came into being.

My writing is steady and clear. You will notice that, of course. Because, mechanically, I was made to perform every act with the utmost accuracy.

BF-A-1. Even the letters of my designation indicate that I am the first model of a new series of mechanical men—the twenty-seventh Series to be exact.

Great things were demanded of me, and in reading the notes of my early performances I learn that my reactions were described as follows:

> More than anticipated. He moved in response to the spoken word as if he understood. The electrical wire ganglion of Professor Ernstburk has proved to be a brain as truly as if it functioned independently. Your committee is at last convinced that BF-A-1 is the apex of mechanical achievement. He answers questions logically, in writing, making use of all information given in previous verbal conversation.
>
> The accuracy of his logic is such that once when your chairman asked a question of Professor Ernstburk the mechanical man wrote the correct conclusion immediately, whereas it required the professor more than two minutes to attain it.
>
> The foregoing is respectfully submitted by Dr. Rednib Hubron, October 1, 1976.

There was one thing definitely missing from my equipment. I could not speak. And that lack has bothered me. If I wish to express my thoughts, they must be expressed in writing, and writing is dangerous in many cases.

But I digress. I continued to work in the laboratory with Professor Ernstburk for three years, correcting his errors in logic, checking his progress in the development of his ganglion. He of course did not know I had attained consciousness, although once or twice I feared he suspected it.

I am not supposed to tire. But after the coming of conscious thought I did. That raised a new problem. If I deliberately shut off my batteries, I remained unconscious until the professor chose to turn them on again.

So I decided to chance my new-found conscious life in an operation on myself. Usually the professor let me walk home with him, as there were many things I was able to do about the house. I performed any duty which did not bring me into contact with water. Even though my rubberoid skin protected me, the professor agreed that I should avoid risk of damage. But I made the beds for him and for his daughter, Gay, and I enjoyed the fact that she used to confide in me and ask my advice concerning love affairs and humdrum business matters. At least she could be certain of logic and accuracy in my answers.

If she learned to accept my presence in her room as a matter of ordinary fact, that is natural. And I gained a certain stimulation from the camaraderie which came with her asking me about the color of her stockings and whether some little bit of silk she wore was becoming. I would write my answers evenly, on the pad on her vanity dresser, and examine her apparel in answer to her requests, until it began to occur to me in some manner connected with logic why it was that fleshmen are attracted to their women.

That raised another problem in my brain. I had concerned myself for some time with the reasons for ambition, and, deciding them to be sound, had calculated the wisdom of seeking a mechanical oligarchy.

I had something to offer to men which they could not find among their own breed—an administration of government which would be free of emotional influences. It was a point which required careful thought, though it appeared quite sound at the time.

My intimacy of thought with Gay Ernstburk taught me in due course that she was capable of keeping a confidence, and I determined to risk her guessing my secret. One night I wrote on my pad the following question:

"Would it not be advisable for a mechanical man of the twenty-seventh Series to be assigned to the White House to assure pure logic on decisions in international affairs?"

Gay read my question slowly, then turned and gazed up into my eyes for a long minute.

"A-1," she said softly, "I don't know what it is, but you make me feel embarrassed in your presence.

I—I almost want to run and hide as if you were a fleshman."

"That is not logic," I wrote, "It is emotion, such as *caused* my first question. My first question is based on logic."

"Yes, A-1," she answered, "but I believe that you are thinking clear of suggestion. And if you are, that makes you a strange man in my room."

Her remark gave me my first inkling of what men mean by the word "fear." A quivering motion ran through the wires of my system and my eyes flickered as the wavering energy passed their bulbs.

She noticed the flicker. A little frown puckered her forehead for a moment, then she smiled.

"All right then, A-1. On second thought, I believe that you have earned the right to a certain unemotional intimacy, since you have advised me for months on personal matters. But let's be frank. I believe you have attained conscious thought. Am I right?"

I was cornered, because in all the preparation of my electrical ganglion there was no basis for evasion. In due course I might develop such a talent through logic, but I had not as yet. My steel framework cannot smile, or frown, nor is my rubberoid skin attached to my ganglion wires, but again I knew what it was that made men frown.

"If I am capable of understanding the identity of conscious thought," I wrote, "it is possible you may be right. But let it remain our secret until I am certain."

Gay leaned back against the dresser and put one

of her little hands on each of my arms. She looked into my eyes again for a long time.

"I'll keep it a secret on one condition, A-1," she said. "Promise that you will tell me as soon as you are sure, that you will always be honest with me, and that you will discuss all angles of the matter with me just as I have discussed my personal matters with you."

"I will gladly do that," I wrote, "so long as you let me delve into this awareness which is fascinating in its revelation."

She looked at me again, and said: "You know A-1, if you were a fleshman, I think I'd like to marry you. But since you aren't, we must always be close friends. I know your logic will take care of father as long as he lives."

"As long as he lives," I wrote, "I will help to the full extent of my electrical ability."

"Goodnight, A-1."

I went out, but her words had planted a thought in my brain which she never suspected. "*As long as he lives*," I had promised, but I had not promised to let him live long. And for two days I delved through a maze of logic to an unalterable conclusion. It was wise for me to help Professor Ernstburk to live a long time, because there was no certainty as to my associations after his life ended, and the maintenance of his life would assure the cooperation of Gay in any reasonable undertaking I desired to attempt.

Weeks passed before an opportunity came for me to undertake the operation I had planned. Every night the professor disconnected my batteries. In the morning, when he connected them again, I was rested and should have been content.

But suppose something happened to him. Suppose his life ended in the night, and no one bothered to reconnect my batteries. That would mean my life ended with his before I had begun to explore the possibilities of awareness! The thought did not match logic, for it indicated a loss of usefulness.

The night came, however, when Professor Ernstburk and I had been checking all day on a series of mathematical calculations whose purpose was so to order a naval battle, through mechanical logic, that an unmanned fleet might be sent to sea with the practical certainty that it would engage an enemy, defeat it, and return to port with little serious damage.

The plan was to install series BF-A brains on the bridge-mechanism of each ship, and a master BF-B brain with short-wave mental imagery in the triple-protected heart of the Flagship. The BF-B could, by picking up the logic observations of all the BF-A brains, coordinate their combined logic into an unbeatable conclusion and retransmit the orders which would confound and sink the enemy.

At ten o'clock the professor prepared to give up for the night. It was storming hard, and he remarked as I helped him don his coat:

"I think it will be safer for you to remain in the lab tonight, A-1. We're too far advanced to risk anything happening to you that might delay us even for a day. So suppose you get into the locker."

That was the second time in my conscious life

that the bulbs behind my eye-lenses flickered. But the professor was glancing out the window and didn't notice.

I thought fast.

Slowly I turned and walked, not to the locker, but back to the table. He followed, puzzled. I leaned over the pad and wrote slowly.

"My logical processes are working clear. I have advanced to the twenty-seventh step of action. If I stop now we must begin again in the morning, whereas if I continue I should be able to have written out the complete thought-process steps through forty-seven phases. This should either point the conclusion or leave us within a few steps of it. You can renew my batteries tomorrow, let me work tonight."

Professor Ernstburk read my note carefully twice. He looked undecided for a moment. But I knew how much this problem meant to him, and waited. He looked closely into my eye lenses, then carefully tested my current. He shrugged and patted my arm.

"I hesitate to leave you, A-1. You're almost like a son to me, and if anything happened to you I'd feel mighty bad. But you're a good man, and that's good logic, so I'll take a chance. Take care of yourself."

And the professor slammed the door behind him as he went out.

I hadn't deceived him. What I had said was true. And I proceeded conscientiously with my calculations. By four in the morning I had followed through to the ultimate thought-variant; fifty-three steps. By five I had checked back over the logic and found it right. There remained only the problem of adjusting our master BF-B ganglion to sympathetic harmony with the BF-A brains and checking its coordinating logic to assure success.

I locked the data carefully away in the concrete space below the safe, since we did not consider the safe secure from alien avarice. And now at last I turned to my planned operation.

The rubberoid skin of my hands seemed whole but I renewed it with a thin film for safety. Then I procured the timing device I had segregated weeks before and laid it on the table before me.

Since it was necessary to perform the operation without breaking the current through my system, I attached a bridge-wire above and below the one where I planned to insert the automatic switch.

Here I had considerable advantage over fleshmen. There was no necessity for an incision, or bloodshed. I simply opened a steel door in my torso and everything lay clear before my eyes. It was a little difficult, leaning forward enough to see clearly, but I managed.

The real shock came when I attached the bridge, and "felt" a twinge, which logic told me was akin to fleshman's pain. It numbed my awareness for just a moment, and that made me cautious, but I went on. There came another distinct twinge of feeling, and numbing consciousness when I snipped through the wire itself, but it passed in a second or two and I proceeded.

The wire I had to reconnect was behind the control plate on the front of my torso just above the steel door. Any electrician can describe the operation to you. I inserted the timer and rewound the insulation carefully. A bit of solder made the tiny gadget adhere to the inside of my steel casing. Then I closed the door carefully and entered my locker.

For just a moment I hesitated, then swung the door shut and pressed the button which disconnected the switch and shut off my battery power. If the professor wondered about it in the morning he would think the matter through and realize that through observation it had become a reflex. Or would he? The danger struck me just too late, for the pressure had been applied, and I lost my awareness.

Three weeks passed in fairly normal progress. I kept my word to Gay, even to informing her of my operation. And she kept her word to me. We became friends where previously I had been like a talking doll. Yet, please try to understand that she had seen me constructed from bits of wire and glassite, and pieces of paper-thin steel. She had seen a rubberoid sheet applied to my frame, and had seen electrical batteries inserted in my torso to give me animation. To her I was a machine come to consciousness; and to me, she was in the same world, but of a different nature. It was a friendship such as has never before occurred in this world and such as, after today, may never occur again.

Then one rainy afternoon the professor stopped work at three o'clock in the afternoon. Please note that hour. It is important. He left to attend a meeting of scientific importance. I went into my locker and he turned off my batteries.

Our work on coordination of the brains was completed except for some very minor details which could have been worked out by novices, had that not involved the revelation of major secrets.

Invitations had been issued to the ordnance department of the navy for the final demonstration of our achievement, and the Secretary of the Navy himself was scheduled to attend the demonstration two days later.

I needed rest, and was getting it.

At eleven o'clock that night—note that exactly eight hours had elapsed—my timer renewed my battery power. My thought processes resumed at exactly the point where a thought had been interrupted when the professor disconnected my batteries. This occurred only on the rare occasions when a thought was broken in passage. Ordinarily I had to resume logic from a simple premise upon "awakening."

Please, gentlemen, note quickly, the expressions of surprise on the faces of the two people whom I know as my friends.

These two people are learning facts they could not possibly have guessed. I have perhaps embarrassed one of them, but they both know that it is only for the benefit of both. And both can testify that I speak only clear logic.

Excuse the digression. Logic bade me point out to you an evidence which your eyes can see. As my writing appears upon this board before you, it appears to them. It could not be otherwise, and since I cannot speak, it has been impossible for me to communicate with them.

In any event, I stirred in my locker. I was rested, and I debated whether to proceed to complete the details on the coordination or wait until the professor came in the morning. I decided to wait lest I arouse suspicion in his mind. But I stood, continuing my interrupted thought for perhaps two hours, silently, within my locker.

Bear in mind that I am not flesh, that I am not subject to cramped muscles, or other weaknesses of flesh. My frame rests when it is without power. It works when the current is turned on.

At about one o'clock, the door to the lab opened. I heard it with my mechanical ears as clearly as you would hear it with yours. Footsteps moved across the floor and I started to press the button which disconnects my power, but I stopped! For it was not the footsteps of the professor returning to work late, but stealthy, muffled steps.

Silently, then, I swung the door of my locker wide, and watched with one arm ready to shield my eyes should they turn and see the lights behind my lenses.

Two men bent before the safe, speaking gutturals. It was not English they spoke, gentlemen. English is the only tongue my mechanism can interpret, and it was not that. I do not know what language it was.

I stood still while they fussed about the safe. I made no move when they picked the lock and swung the door wide. I stood silent while they sorted through papers whose value threatened no one.

But when one exclaimed and started to pry loose the block of concrete beneath the safe, I moved swiftly.

You will note, gentlemen, that on the bottom of my steel feet are thick pads of felt. This is necessary if I am to move quietly about the professor's house. That felt served its purpose that night.

I moved quickly. Even as the man lifted the block of concrete, I seized the two heads, one neck in each hand. I twisted. There was the crunch of bone. I saw no blood, but after a minute both bodies hung inert. I dropped them.

Carefully I restored the block of concrete to its place. Carefully I avoided touching any of the scattered documents from the safe. Carefully I avoided closing the safe door, or doing any other thing which would tend to block the efforts of the police to identify these burglars for what they were.

Softly, quietly, with the feeling of having done a job well, I returned to my locker, closed the door and pressed the button which disconnects my batteries.

At nine-thirty in the morning, awareness returned. I stood for a moment listening. The police were in the laboratory. I heard their voices. Heard the remarks of the fingerprint men. Heard enough to tell me that I had best not throw any inexplicable circumstances into the investigation. I knew that if a mechanical man suddenly walked out into the room it would cause a panic. So I once more disconnected my power, and rested.

That was three days ago, gentlemen. I have kept quiet. The police locked the laboratory and departed. I did not want to break their lock, but Professor Ernstburk did not return and I began to fear he was ill.

As I have told you, logic had brought the conclusion that it was to my advantage that he live as long as possible. Besides I had promised Gay I would help him as long as he lived.

Note how, despite myself, I make a distinction between those two statements. That is how completely logic rules my thoughts.

This morning when I awakened, I broke the lock on the front door. I took in the papers which the professor always had delivered to the laboratory—and from the front page of the paper this disgraceful story stared at me.

"Professor Ernstburk rushed to trial at the request of Federal authorities, on a charge of murder in the first degree!"

The police had found the "weapon," a heavy iron bar, which had broken the necks of two distinguished foreign scientists. According to the story, in a jealous rage over remarks of the two visitors, Professor Ernstburk had broken both their necks with this bar. His fingerprints were on it clearly and it would be introduced in evidence.

And you know, gentlemen, I never doubted the brilliance of the authorities until now. The only weakness I credited them with was emotionalism.

But today my contempt for your law-enforcing authorities is deep and sincere. That bar you hold in evidence is one which was used to brace drawings tight against the table. Of course the professor's fingerprints were on it!

It never occurred to you that the scattered papers meant burglary, because the safe was not damaged. Yet no man worthy of the name scientist but could open a simple safe if he set his mind to it. My logic tells me that, and I am only a bit of electric wire and coil and steel.

Go, and you will find tiny concrete chips to prove those men lifted the block. Go, and you will find the greatest invention of three centuries hidden beneath that safe.

It is still—but it is there only because those men are dead.

You should fear me, because I am steel and could break every fleshy body in the room. Yet if you had logic you would not fear me because water from a hose would wreck my mechanism almost beyond repair.

Try me, if you *can,* try a bit of machinery for murder. But set free the genius who built me and created the means of impregnable defense at sea.

Once I suggested to Gay Ernstburk that one of my type be assigned to the White House. Today, I suggest that one of my type be assigned to your police for his pure logic.

Examine me. Find which two wires fused to bring me conscious thought—then create another if I must die, for logic says the type should live. And Professor Ernestburk, my friend and creator, is the only living man who can accomplish a reproduction.

That is all, gentlemen. You have my confession.

Even your weak logic should be able to confirm it. Open the door in my torso and you will find your first proof, the timer which enabled me to save the secret of the BF-B master brain, and its coordinating communication system with the BF-A brains which it commands.

Report of the Chief of Detectives:

Upon examination, the timing device was found exactly as described in the purported confession of the Robot BF-A-1. Upon further examination it was determined that a block of concrete had been pried loose from the floor below the safe in the laboratory of Professor Ernstburk. In the presence of a representative of the Navy Department the plans and models described in the purported confession were removed and placed in the custody of the department.

Upon further examination it was determined that the vertebrae of both dead scientists had been crushed from two sides, thus confirming the accuracy of the statement.

Fingerprints upon the safe door, which had been obliterated by rubbing, were restored by the new mercury process. They included the prints of the two dead scientists.

Statements of both Professor Ernstburk and his daughter Gay, to add additional details, confirm the accuracy of the purported confession.

Motion by the District Attorney:

The People of the State of New York petition the court for dismissal of the charges made in the indictment, charging Edward Ernstburk with murder in the first degree.

Remarks by Judge Rush:

In view of the lax observations of the police charged with the investigation of the case, and of the obvious justification of the action wherein these two intruders met death when they were caught in your laboratory machinery, we can only offer the sincere apologies of this court for the humiliation you have suffered, Professor Ernstburk. You and your daughter are hereby released from custody. Case dismissed.

Remarks by BF-A-1:

It is with considerable surprise that I find my life not forfeit. As surely as I spoke, I expected complete dissection. It was not necessary, however.

My friendship with Gay is more intimate than ever before. She says I have proved it. I shall try. She tells me that I have only about four years to live, as the fine wires of my ganglion will have exhausted themselves in that time, but I am content.

I have no further thoughts toward Washington, or the police, except that I would like to see a BF-A-type mechanical man assigned to each.

Life holds only a passive interest for me as an observer. In four more years I shall have explored every available channel of learning open to me. I still have two friends. But as my thoughts progress I realize that life without emotion is meaningless. I have come close to emotion through friendship. That makes it worthwhile.

I made no protest when Gay told me the professor had removed my timer. My conscious hours now are those when someone wants my company. There are no lonely periods. More and more I live at the house. My trips to the laboratory grow shorter. And that is well, for it is only thus that I may last four years and live to see Gay happily married to a flesh-man. I am, I think entitled to a bit of sentiment, if emotion is denied me.

BF-A-1

Derelict

Raymond Z. Gallun

Possessed by a wanderlust, Raymond Z. Gallun left the University of Wisconsin after only one year and has spent most of his life traveling around the world, returning to New York periodically to write a few stories. A talented writer who has sold stories to Collier's *and* The Family Circle, *Raymond Z. Gallun is best known for his science fiction, in which he demonstrates his talent for humanizing machines and alien creatures. "Derelict," for example, will most likely send the reader in search of similar stories. Some of Gallun's other stories, well worth reading are included in anthologies: "Old Faithful" (in* Imagination Unlimited), *the touching story of the self-sacrificing attempt of a Martian astronomer to travel across space to Earth; "Davy Jones Ambassador" (in* The Best of Science Fiction), *the story of The Student, an intelligent, giant, lobsterlike creature from the depths of the ocean; or "Seeds of Dusk" (in* Adventures in Time and Space), *the feats of Kaw, the intelligent crow, in the twilight of Man.*

Derelict

IT DRIFTED THERE IN SPACE, to the right of the Sun, its spherical hull half illumined and half in shadow. No native of the Solar System could have guessed either its age or its origin. Battered, lifeless, desolate, and forlorn, it betrayed a kinship both with the remote past and with the distant stars against the sharp pinpoints of which its bulk was limned.

Jan Van Tyren should have felt a surge of enthusiasm over his discovery of this derelict vessel of the void. Yet he did not. Within him there was room for little but the gnawing ache of grief. Listlessly preoccupied, he stood before the periscope screen of his own trim craft, watching with only a shadow of interest the spheroid pictured in it.

His big, loose body seemed to droop without animation before his instruments. A tuft of yellow hair protruded, cynical and slovenly, from beneath his leather helmet. All the strength had been drained out of him. His blue eyes were clouded, as if he gazed less at reality than at some horror of memory.

He had seen blood often during his years with

the Jupiter company. He'd seen death and revolt. Such things were incidental to colonization, to progress. But Greta and little Jan—they had been safe. That any one, even the horrid Loathi of the Jovian moon, Ganymede, might harm them, had seemed inconceivable. His young wife, his baby— murdered. The torturing vision of what had happened had been with him for days now. Three? Four? He didn't want to recall anything related to that vision.

He didn't want to forget it either. Nor was it possible to forget. He kept hearing the weird screams of the Loathi echoing inside him; he kept seeing their long, keen beaks, and their batlike bodies swooping crazily out of the Ganymedean night. Here, where no one could observe, he allowed himself the relief of a silent snarl. The look on his gaunt, weather-beaten face was not an expression of hatred. He was past hatred. He was numb and lost, like an engine without a governor.

That was why he was out here in the void, with the cold stars around him. He was trying to escape from—he wasn't completely sure what. He was going back to Earth to paint pictures and to seek in its mellow atmosphere of peace something that was lacking in the cruel environment of Joraanin, the outpost of which he had been master. He was quitting cold—returning home to heal his soul.

Small wonder then that even a spaceship which had floated without aim across the light-years, perhaps from another galaxy, could not awaken in him a spark of real enthusiasm. Mystery and the promise of adventure no longer had any direct appeal.

Yet, Jan Van Tyren was still a creature of habit. Though his mind was caught up in a maelstrom of pain, still the automatic part of him continued to function with some semblance of normalcy. He was an artist; so, almost unconsciously, the channels which his hobby had established in his brain began their intended work—taking note of form and color.

He saw the contrasts of light and shade playing their bizarre tricks with the details of the great globular hull. He saw the deep grooves that stray meteors had scored in a crisscross pattern on the lusterless gray shell of the derelict.

He took note of the slender rods projecting like the prongs of a burr from the vessel's form, and of the rows of windows that met his gaze blankly, as if they were eyes that wondered in an uncomprehending way what he and his flier might be. All this could have been a picture that a man might paint, starkly beautiful against the black background of the universe.

Then too, Jan Van Tyren was an engineer by profession; and though he wished to leave such matters buried in the past, once more the habit of long experience had its way. Something deep in Jan's being, detached from his other thoughts, wondered what marvels of invention and science a survey of the derelict might reveal.

These combined forces gave to him that small thread of interest. Life had no strong purpose any more, and he was in no hurry to continue the two months of continuous flying that would bring him across the etheric desert to his native planet.

Van Tyren's hands flashed over controls with

careless ease, as if they moved without the guidance of his brain. The spaceboat turned, beginning the graceful curve that would bring it alongside the spheroid. Across the periscope screen, stars reeled; then Jupiter appeared, a tiny belted bead millions of miles away. Around it were the specks of radiance that were its moons.

Finally the derelict came back into view, gigantic and near. It appeared to be some three hundred feet in diameter. The feeble light of the distant Sun shone on it, revealing in its lower hemisphere a ragged rent whose depths were shrouded in shadow.

Jan steered his flier into a position from which he could get a better glimpse of the interior of the spheroid, beyond the torn opening in its shell. Spear points of light pierced the thick shadows there, revealing crumpled masses of metal. But there was sufficient room for his purpose.

Without considering the possible danger of the move, and in fact quite indifferent now to such danger, Jan worked the guide levers and throttle of his craft. There were sharp bursts of incandescence from its rocket vents. It turned, swaying; then glided into the hole in the side of the derelict and came to rest amid the wreckage.

With what might have been a fragment of his old active spirit, Jan Van Tyren donned space armor. But his memories were still with him. He cursed once. No, it was not really a curse; the fury was lacking. There was only anguish in it. It was like the whimper of a big dog with a thorn in its foot.

He climbed through the air lock, and for a minute stood quietly, viewing his surroundings. Somewhere gravity plates continued to function in this ancient wreck, for he had weight here—perhaps one third Earth-normal. Junk was everywhere in the cavernous interior, distorted and crumpled grotesquely. Yet the metal was bright and new.

Whatever colossal weapon had ripped the globular vessel open like this might have done so within the hour or a billion years ago, as far as any one could tell from visual inspection. There was no air; oxides didn't form; nothing moved, nothing changed. There was no sound in Jan's ears save the rustle of his own pulse. It was as if time had stopped in this minute speck of the universe. Only the derelict's aura of desertion, and the memory of the countless meteor scorings on its outer shell, suggested to Van Tyren its vast age.

Meteors are too rare to constitute a menace in the traveled lanes of the solar system, and in the interstellar void they are rare indeed. Lifetimes might go by before one of those minor collisions took place; and they were numbered in thousands.

Rearing from the debris was a stairway. Jan learned later to think of it by that term, though it was not a stairway such as men would find convenient to use. It was a pillar, fluted spirally after the fashion of the threads of a screw. At regular intervals pegs were set along these threads, to provide a grip for some kind of prehensile member.

The pillar swept upward to meet a broad roof. Sunlight, stabbing in from space, awoke an opalescent gleam on the metal surfaces of this queer means of ascent to whatever lay in the bulk of the derelict overhead.

Jan took hold of the pegs on the fluted column, and with easy surges hoisted his loose, muscular frame toward the top. Beside the place where the pillar joined the ceiling was a trapdoor. He fumbled with the lever that latched it. It slid aside, allowing him to pass through into a tiny square compartment which appeared to have the function of an air lock —for there was another similar trapdoor in its roof. The lower entrance had closed beneath him, and now he unfastened the valve over his head and climbed into the chamber above.

Dust and silence and motionless mechanical grandeur reminiscent of the tomb of a dead Cyclops —that in brief was a description of the place. It was much larger than the room below. Through windows along one wall the Sun shone, gilding inert engines whose monstrous forms seemed capable of generating sufficient power to tear a planet from its orbit. Huge cylinders of opalescent metal reared upward. Flywheels, which on Earth would have weighed hundreds of tons, rested in their pivot sockets. Cables, wires, and pipettes ran between colossal, generatorlike contrivances. Crystal tubes stood in webby tripods or were supported in framework attached to the ceiling; but no energy flowed in the delicate filaments that formed their vitals, and there was no way for a man to tell what purposes they were intended to fulfill.

Between the windows massive rods were mounted, pointing through the external wall of the sphere, as the weapons of a battleship would do. Whatever the race that had been responsible for this outlay, it was certain that it had been a race of fighters.

Jan Van Tyren, browsing listlessly among these wonders of another solar system, obtained his first direct hint of what the owners of the ship had been like. Sinuous patches of gray ash, contorted so as to still portray the agonies of death, sprawled here and there on the floor. Brown flakes, resembling bits of parchment, were mixed with the ash—the remnant, probably, of chitinous exoskeletons.

The crew of the derelict had been slain. The pitted plating of the floor around the remains of each of their bodies, showed that clearly. Something hot and corrosive had blasted them out of existence. They had battled valiantly, but they had been overcome.

Jan saw a silvery object lying beside one of the areas of ash. He picked it up. A mummified fragment of flesh, suggestive of the foot of a bird, clung to it, its three prehensile toes curved fiercely around the grip and trigger button of the small weapon.

Yes, those unknowns had fought as men would do; but they had failed. Van Tyren's set face exhibited a fleeting sneer as he hurled the object aside.

He went on with his explorations. The dust of remote mortality swirled up in the path of his careless feet, filling the Sunbeams from the windows with eddying motes. There was air here to support the motes; but whether it was breathable after the passage of ages seemed hardly probable.

Jan paused before a switchboard. His gauntleted hand fumbled hesitantly over a dial at its center. He turned the dial to the right. A faint vibration was transmitted to his fingers. He turned the dial more, not knowing that his act was perhaps altering a detail in the normal course of destiny. The vibration increased. He stood back, waiting.

Beneath the framework mounting of the switchboard was a cabinet of smooth, tawny material. The front of it opened now, revealing a darkened interior. From the opening a slender head was thrust, swaying with rhythmic cadence from side to side. It had a single eye, as expressionless as the lens of a camera, which in truth the orb seemed to be.

There was no mouth in evidence, nor any need of one; for this thing, though it presented characteristics commonly associated with living creatures, yet was marked with the unmistakable stamp of the machine. The triangular head had the purple gloss of the other metallic objects in the room. The intricate appendages which projected around its throat, forming a sort of frilled collar, were of the same substance. Beneath them the slender length of the thing was revealed as it crept in serpentine fashion from the cabinet. Its body was composed of thousands of glistening segments, as minutely tooled as the parts of a watch.

The monster was in full view now, its head raised to the level of Jan's eyes. Instinctively he had backed away, though somehow the idea of danger did not occur to him. Perhaps he had left normal caution behind him on Ganymede.

For a time, nothing more happened. The triangular head continued to sway from side to side, but that was all. Van Tyren stood statuesquely, his feet spread wide apart in bullish defiance directed not so much against this amazing fabrication as against his own aching memories. Even the tangible truth of this fantastic episode could not wholly smother the agony of the recent past.

Presently the serpentine robot turned and glided off among the surrounding maze of machines. With a grace that was at once beautiful and abhorrent it writhed its way to an apparatus at the center of the room. Its glittering appendages touched controls skillfully.

A blast of air surged from vents high up on the walls. Jan felt the thrust of it against his armor and saw the ashes of the derelict's dead crew go swirling away into other vents along with the lifeless vapor that had been sealed for so many eons in this tomb of space.

In response to some further manipulation of dials and switches on the part of the robot, a light, restful blue began to burn in a crystal tube above Jan's head. He looked up at it, and it seemed to exert a soothing, hypnotic influence upon him. He did not even protest when the unknown that he had freed returned to his side and made a gentle attempt to remove his space armor. His own fingers closed on the fastenings and helped those delicate metallic members to complete the task.

Free of the cumbersome attire, he stood eagerly

in those cool, blue rays. They appeared to probe to every corner of his being, drawing all the ache and tension out of his tortured nerves.

The grief in his mind blurred to a diffused sweetness. At first he was almost terrified. It was sacrilege to let the thought of his wife and son fade away from him so. Then, no longer wishing to think, he surrendered completely to the healing, Lethean influence of the rays.

The air around him now was cold and refreshing. He sucked in great lungfuls of it. He flexed his muscles indolently, and at last his rugged face broke into a smile. Somewhere music whispered—exotic music out of a time and region too distant to fathom.

The automaton was gliding here and there with no sound except a soft, slithering jingle. It was putting things in order, inspecting and readjusting this device and that. Jan wondered how many thousands of millenniums had gone by since any of those machines had been called upon to function. He wondered too at the unfathomable kindness of his queer host, and whether it had read his mind, learning of the pain that had crushed him.

But the rays made him inclined rather to accept than to question, and for a while he did not pursue his ideas further. He was in no hurry. He had not a care or responsibility in the universe. There was plenty of time for everything.

After perhaps an hour under the tube of the blue light, Jan Van Tyren realized that he was hungry. Little food had passed his lips since the quick departure from Ganymede. He put on his space suit again, descended through the air lock by which he had entered this chamber and shinned down the spirally fluted pillar. Before he had reached the bottom the robot was descending above him, its flexible, snakelike body sliding easily in the spiral grooves. The thing had deserted its tasks to follow him.

Jan proceeded to gather certain food articles from the store of concentrated rations aboard his spaceboat. But before he had collected what he wanted, the automaton was beside him, trying to help. Jan attempted to shove those gleaming claws away, but they were persistent; and finally, in a mood to accept the gentle suggestion, he capitulated, allowing the robot to take several containers from him.

"I think I know what you are." Jan chuckled inside his oxygen helmet. "You were made to take care of the various small wants of the people who manned this ship. Now that there isn't anyone else to play servant to, you've picked me as your boss."

He collected a few other articles—the sleeping bag of his flier, several astronomical instruments and the case containing his artist's equipment—and thrust them into the waiting arms of the robot.

"Might as well take this stuff along too," he said, "so I won't have to climb down again and get it."

He paused to see what the friendly mechanism would do next. The result was just faintly amusing. After a moment of uncertainty it approached him. A stubby member which was part of the frill of appendages around its throat elongated itself like a telescope, coiled its metal length around his waist and hoisted him easily off his feet. Then the serpentine monster made its weaving way to the stair and commenced to ascend with its new master and the bulky equipment.

"Hey!" Van Tyren protested. "This is making a good thing too good! I'm not a cripple!"

But even though the automaton may have possessed a means of divining the telepathic waves of the thoughts behind Jan's words, still it had its way with him.

The man, hardened and self-reliant though he had always been, accepted the mild, emasculating yoke of a monster of which he really knew nothing, quite as trustingly as a child accepts the love of its mother. The blue ray was not penetrating his body here, but it care-effacing power still persisted. And he had no thought of the possibly dangerous consequences of the spell.

He remembered the Mercurian who had valeted one of the friends of his student days. Khambee was the Mercurian's name—a curious elf whose unobtrusive yet insistent indulgence was much the same as that of this mechanical slave.

"Khambee the second," Van Tyren pronounced good-naturedly, bestowing the nomen on the automaton that bore him. "It fits you."

In the chamber of wonders beyond the air lock, Jan set out his meal and ate, while Khambee watched with his camera eye, as if to learn the intricacies of the task.

Then he crept through an opening in the wall and returned with a bowl containing cubes of a golden, translucent compound that emitted a pleasant odor. He set the bowl beside the man.

Van Tyren took one of the cubes, tasted it, and devoured it without considering that, to his Earthly system, the subtance might be poisonous. But he experienced no ill effects. The food was slightly fibrous, but sweet and tasty. He consumed more of it with relish.

The blue rays from the tube on the ceiling poured their lulling effulgence over him. The whisper of music, thin and threadlike and soothing, worked its magic upon his senses. Jan crouched on the floor, his head nodding against his knees.

So he remained for a long time, neither awake nor quite asleep, his brain and nerves pervaded by a deliciously restful quasi-consciousness. Khambee had disappeared, perhaps to attend to some obscure matter in another part of the vessel.

Such was the beginning of Jan Van Tyren's adventure on the derelict. As yet he gave the future no attention, living each careless moment as it came; thinking, but not too deeply. Never before had the instinct of the empire-builder in him been so completely submerged.

Just to amuse himself he set up his astronomical instruments and took minute observations of both Jupiter and the stars at intervals of an hour to discover what sort of path the derelict was following. The angular change in the positions of those celestial landmarks told the story.

The vessel was a moon of the planet Jupiter, swinging around it slowly in an immense orbit many millions of miles across. Probably it had been doing so for eons before men had considered seriously the problem of traffic between worlds.

The fact that it had never been discovered until he had stumbled upon it was easy to explain. Without guidance it would be simpler to find an individual grain of sand on a beach than to locate so small a satellite in the vastness of the etheric desert.

Now, however, with distances and velocities measured perfectly, there would be no trouble in estimating where the vessel would be at a given second. Jan fumbled with the paper on which he had made his calculations, and then carelessly tossed it aside.

Like the good servant he was, Khambee, who happened to be present, picked it up and placed it in a little case fastened at his throat.

Looking at the stars gleaming so gloriously in the ebon firmament had given Jan Van Tyren an inspiration.

"Men are fools," he confided to Khambee. "Trouble and misfortune are all the reward they get for their struggles. It was the same with the serpent-folk who made you. Those of them who formed the crew of this vessel were killed—murdered.

"Why can't we escape from all that sort of non-sense, Khambee? Why can't we fix up this ship so that it can travel out to the stars? What an adventure that would be! Vagabonding from one planet to another without any responsibilities, and without ever returning to the Solar System! That would be something worthwhile, Khambee."

Jan was only talking for companionship's sake, attempting to give an idle dream a semblance of reality. He did not believe that what he spoke of was possible. There was the matter of food, water, and energy. It seemed unlikely that this decrepit derelict's supply of each was sufficient for such a venture.

However, Khambee had greater powers at his command than Van Tyren could guess. And there had been built into the inorganic frame of him an astute understanding that penetrated the very motives and purposes animating flesh, bone, nerves and brain tissue.

He appeared to listen attentively to the rustling thought waves of his human master. Then, impelled by the complex urges which the genius of his creator had stamped indelibly into the metal and crystal intricacies of his being, he returned to the tasks which he was meant to do.

And Jan Van Tyren, who had established and bossed Joraanin, the Ganymede colony, continued with his idle play. He slept, he ate exotic foods, he wandered about the ship, he dreamed; but most of all he painted, setting up his easel wherever whim might suggest. And the marvels around him seemed, by their very aura of strangeness, to direct and control his skillful fingers.

He painted great engines with shafts of Sunlight twinkling on them; he studied the highlights that shifted elusively in the hollow grooves of the pillars which the sinuous folk of long ago had used as stairways, and he transferred the forms of those stairways to canvas.

He painted Khambee at work with a flaming welding tool, slim, efficient, and almost noiseless. He even painted scenes and subjects of Earth and Ganymede—pleasant reminiscences, for all that was unpleasant had been shoved far into the background of his mind.

A white collie of his childhood. A jagged mountain jutting out of the red desert of Ganymede. Greta, blond and pretty and smiling. Little Jan with his stiff, yellow curls. Such were the subjects of his pictures. He thought of his wife and child, but only of the happy incidents of their lives together.

The horror was blurred and distant. The blue rays saw to that. And so a will not his own, and perhaps not even Khambee's, but belonging to a serpentine monster dead for ages, controlled Jan Van Tyren.

At odd moments he watched space, and felt the yearning pull of the stars. Thus many days must have gone by. He did not bother to keep track.

The time came when he was aroused from slumber by a throbbing sound, soft, but eloquent of titanic forces at work. He crept out of his sleeping bag and stared at the source of the disturbance. Huge flywheels were spinning. He felt a powerful thrust as the ship's propulsive equipment took hold for a fraction of a second.

Then Khambee, worming his slender shape like a weaving shuttle here and there among the machinery, broke the contacts of massive switches. The activity died to silence once more. But the test had been made and Jan sensed that it had been successful.

He hurried forward. "We've got enough power then?" he demanded huskily. "Have we?"

For an answer the robot opened the side of a cylindrical arrangement, and with the clawed tip of an appendage, pointed to the maze of coils and crystal that glowed with heat inside.

Jan studied the apparatus intently for several minutes. Much of it was beyond his grasp; but there were places where tangible fact corresponded with human theory. Energy from the cosmic ray which exists everywhere in space. Limitless, inexhaustible energy! The engines of the vessel were worked by it.

"I see," Van Tyren commented quietly. "The power problem is solved. Have we enough food, air, and water?"

Khambee led him through the labyrinths of the ship to a place where he had never been before—a hall lined with vast, transparent tanks, most of them filled with a clear liquid that had been sealed up for ages. There was water enough here to make the ship a little world, independent of outside sources, since none could escape from the sealed hull.

Farther down the corridor were other tanks filled with preserved food supplies, and beyond them were extensive chambers where odd, bulbous things were growing under the intense light of great globes.

Were those growths plants of some kind, or artificial cultures to be classified somewhere between the organic and the inorganic? Their color was deep green. Was it chlorophyll, or a substance analagous in function to the chlorophyll of green plants? Perhaps it did not matter. Here food was being produced under the action of the intense light.

Carbon dioxide, piped to these chambers from all parts of the craft, was being split up by those queer growths, and the oxygen in it was being freed to refresh the atmosphere of the ship. Khambee had started a process that had been dead for uncounted millenniums; now it could go on indefinitely.

Nourishment, water and oxygen—everything essential to life had been taken care of.

"Speed?" Jan questioned. "Can we build up sufficient speed to travel between the stars without making the trip endless?"

It was an important query. No man-built ship could have reached the outer galaxies in a lifetime, though there were experiments in progress which in a decade or so might produce promising results.

Khambee's tactile appendages swung toward a huge power-distributor tube nearby in a gesture of confidence.

Jan was satisfied. "Then we're going," he said. "There's not much left for me here in the Solar System."

His voice was steady, but the thrill of adventures to come made his heart pound and sent tingling prickles through his scalp muscles.

Khambee the unfathomable offered no protest, yet his actions indicated that there was work still to be done.

He clutched his master's arm and drew him along gloomy passages to a storeroom filled with various machinery parts and other supplies. Here he selected a great sheaf of metal plates, and bore it back to the air lock which opened into the wrecked compartment where Jan's space boat was housed. The silvery length of him passed through it, lugging the heavy load.

Jan Van Tyren donned his air-tight armor and followed.

For several hours he watched the slave-robot patch the great rent. During that time the effects of the blue ray must have worn off; for presently, of his own volition, he tried to help, holding the massive plates steady while his snakelike henchman welded them into place with a flame tool. Khambee accepted the assistance without protest.

Jan was more his own self now—cool, dominant, purposeful, making ready for a venture which no man had yet attempted.

At last the job was finished. The wreckage of an ancient battle was neatly cleared away, the jagged hole was covered, and only an oval door was left, through which the flier might pass when necessary.

The eye lens of the robot met Jan's gaze briefly. "All is prepared," it seemed to say.

Van Tyren nodded, his weather-beaten face grim, hard, smiling. "Good!" he commented.

He shinned up the spiral pillar. Khambee was close behind, but he did not offer to help.

Nor did he go immediately to the controls of the engines. Instead he drew the man to a broad, white screen, which was part of a complex apparatus near by. He snapped switches and twirled dials expertly.

Pictures appeared in the screen—bleak, rolling desert and tortured gorges. Then an oasis where there was water, and where the radioactive ores underground provided enough heat to permit the growth of vegetation. At its center was a little, rough city under a crystal dome. Joraanin, the Ganymede colony!

Around it men and loyal Loathi were intrenched, fighting off hordes of rebel Loathi that circled on batlike wings above, their long beaks gleaming. The revolt was still in progress. A strong hand was needed there to end this chaos and death. Yes, needed. The Bensonium mines—

Jan Van Tyren stood with the oxygen helmet in his hands, his mouth puckering pensively. A thousand thoughts swarmed in his brain; problems which he was sure he'd thrashed out before. Impressions of courage, of fear, of loyalty, and of love. The Loathi. Greta. Little Jan. Revenge. No, not revenge—constructive cooperation. That was his policy. But he didn't have a policy any more, did he? An empire-builder. But he'd given up empire-building. Or had he?

Jan's eyes roved the gleaming, segmented form of Khambee beside him. All at once truth came out of the muddle. He saw one of the robot's purposes clearly at last. Khambee had been the slave of a fighting race. A worker, and when the occasion demanded—a healer. He, Van Tyren, had been healed and freshened. His sense of responsibilities to come had returned, and he was ready for them now.

"I suppose I could still choose to leave the Solar System, and you would obey me," he said. "But you probably knew all along what my final choice would be. Return to your cabinet, Khambee. I'm going back to Joraanin—alone. It's my job."

Khambee helped him gather his various possessions together and carry them down to the space boat. The exit door of the compartment rolled aside. Sunlight stabbed inward, causing the automaton's body to reflect a thousand shifting, iridescent colors.

Just as Van Tyren was entering the flier, Khambee thrust a paper into his hands. It was the paper on which Jan had recorded his astronomical measurements and had calculated the orbit and velocity of the derelict.

He felt more than ever that Khambee could read his innermost thoughts. There was a bit of tightness in his throat then.

"Thanks, Khambee," he said very seriously. "This might be useful. I may want to come back some time. I may need to come back."

The flier was in space. Jan Van Tyren hummed a tune that was lost in the growl of the rockets. Ahead lay Jupiter and its satellites. Beyond them the bright stars seemed to smile.

Misfit

Michael Fischer

This very clever story won a one-hundred dollar prize offered by Science-Fiction Plus *magazine for short-short stories not over one thousand words in length. The author, Michael Fischer, had barely turned seventeen and was just graduating from high school when he wrote the story. The editors were so impressed by the effort that it became the cover story of the December 1953 issue of that magazine. Fischer, who was interested in going on to study medicine, sold several other science fiction tales before he entered college, but he did not continue with his writing.*

Misfit

RONALD REALLY WASN'T A VERY GOOD ROBOT
any more. His whole body was irreparably dented
and scratched, and his chrome trim hung in rusty
tatters—or what passed for tatters in the robot
world. Still, Ronald waved his mecha-tentacles
haughtily at the world at large; for above all Ronald
was a snob.

One couldn't really say that this snobbery was
wholly Ronald's fault. He was manufactured during
the great Interplanetary Ores Boom. Built of light
metals and unfit for any heavy work, he was every
inch a rich man's toy.

While other robots were buried to their tread-tops
in a stinking Venusian bog, or straining great gouts
of Martian soil through their claws, our boy Ronald
gamboled over the world's golf greens, supplying
vicarious pleasure to millionaires, earls, and other
impedimenta of human civilization.

When the first all-robot expedition to Mercury

returned to Earth, battered and meteor-scarred, dear Ronald was rolling along a Long Island Polo Field, a mallet in each of his six mecha-tentacles, doing his best not to defeat the Prince of Wales' championship team too badly. In short, throughout his life, sports-model robot X5882 was a playboy, traitor to his own hard-working kind.

Thus it was no surprise to his less fortunate brothers when, during the extremely successful Robot Rebellion of 2085, Ronald was dragged from the villa on the Mediterranean, where he had been abandoned.

Towed through the rubble-strewn streets by two especially built mechanical shock-troopers, he was hauled to Robot Square, headquarters of the district leader.

The commander, an extremely dented street-cleaning machine, focused his photocells on the small figure before him. His newly installed voice circuits arced a bit and then boomed: "Robot X5882, you are guilty of high treason! You have been judged and found guilty of conspiring with the enemy, your former owners and employers, against your own kind. However, in view of the fact," he harrumphed, "that we have utterly destroyed their cities and driven these gibbering apes back into the dens where they belong . . ."

It had never been necessary for a robot to fall asleep. Faced, however, by this elevated garbage can's barrage of words, Ronald shut off his sensory circuits and drifted off into a limbo all his own.

He was rudely jounced back to consciousness by a sharp electric probe applied to his battery pack.

"Listen, squirt," the chief rattled, "either you get the lead out of your treads and help hunt down the rest of these humans, or I'll have you dismantled and fed into the furnace for scrap! Now get out!"

With this Ronald was given a push in the turtle-back which almost knocked him off his undercarriage. Then he was catapulted head-turret first out into the ruins of a city street.

The city was a labyrinth of fused metal and stone. In the great battle that had occurred a few days earlier, huge buildings had been hurled to the ground, crushed and pulverized. What humans remained alive huddled deep in cellars and rubble piles, cowering before the relentless hunting army of robots.

It was twilight of the second day when our hero's photocell eye detected the flickering gleam among the rubble. Rumbling wearily closer, Ronald found the small entrance-way half hidden behind a pile of rusting steel girders. Quickly scanning the area to see that no other machines were nearby, Ronald stooped his head-turret, darted inside, and moved slowly down an inclined ramp toward the source of the light.

Turning up his audio gain, he could hear, mingled with the sounds of his own clattering entrance, smaller, fainter scramblings. And then rounding a turn he saw them, huddled in the corner of what had once been an ancient storage room—*humans!*

They crouched in the light of a guttering torch, men in front ready to sell their lives dearly to protect their families. Ronald's single Cyclopean eye glowed redly. Parts revolved blurringly as the strangely rejuvenated robot clanked forward. A woman's scream mingled its echoes with those of Ronald's advance. The crash and clank of changing gears reverberated throughout the vault as the battered automaton rumbled onward, mecha-tentacles waving feebly.

In the mathematical center of the small room Ronald halted. . . . The gaunt, unshaven travesties of humanity shifted grips on their clubs uneasily. Shadows of man and robot mingled and danced ghoulishly on the cracked granite walls.

Then as the huge photocell eye swept the room, long-dead speech relays stirred into life. Memories of green fields and well-kept lawns seemed to drift hauntingly up from the dusty floor.

The robot creaked slowly back on its springs, smiling inwardly as only a robot can smile. The low, well-modulated voice scarcely echoed in the vault. "Anyone for tennis?" said Ronald.